A LOST SOUL: THE REVEL[A]

First edition. November 7, 2022.

Copyright © 2022 Miracle Adebiyi.

ISBN: 979-8201414023

Written by Miracle Adebiyi.

Table of Contents

A LOST SOUL
THE REVELATION

MIRACLE ADEBIYI

ISBN: 9798201414023

Foreward

 Set in the period of the rise of the Third Reich and at the moment of Jesse Owens' gold medal winning victories at the 1936 Berlin Olympic Games, Miracle Adebiyi's debut novel is an innovative and imaginative thriller with twists and turns that will keep the reader engaged until its final conclusion. In the vein of Quentin Tarantino's film making, Adebiyi's writing is replete with cultural references and stylised set pieces in its narration of a murder mystery linked to the machinations of the Third Reich.

Dr Justine Baillie
Associate Professor
School of Humanities and Social Sciences
Faculty of Liberal Arts and Sciences

DEDICATION

I dedicate this to my mother and my family.
I love you all very much.

Prologue

IN GERMANY, A NEW TIDE has swept across the people as new ideals and leadership have been decided amongst the well-known Weimar Republic under the rule of Paul von Hindenburg, the president of Germany. A man who goes by the name Adolf Hitler, who led the National Socialist German Workers' Party, which now goes by the name the "Nazi Party", has been appointed Chancellor of a coalition government. His party was the largest in parliament which led to the decision by Hindenburg that Hitler should be second in position to him within the government.

Hitler decides to suspend many civil liberties and begins to allow imprisonment without trial. In March 1933, the first Nazi Concentration Camp is established at Dachau under Hitler's orders as he decided that it was suitable for political dissidents on not only Germany's future but on the faults of the past that needed to be solved. One of these faults Hitler provided was the increase in Jewish communities. Throughout March and the year in 1933, Hitler decided to create further laws to target Jewish communities in Berlin, Hamburg and Munich and other major cities, restricting the jobs they could hold and revoking their German Citizenship. Anti- Semitic sentiment increased as the Jewish population was blamed for the past, including German's defeat in World War One.

Following an increase in power within Germany, Paul von Hindenburg died on 2 August 1934. With the support of the German armed forces, Hitler became President of Germany. Later that month, Hitler began to abolish the office of President and declared himself Führer of the German Reich and People, in addition to his position as Chancellor. In late 1934, towards the end of summer, Jews were subjected to further laws confining their rights. Rising anti-Semitism was not limited to Germany.

Meanwhile, earlier in April in the United Kingdom, a man by the name Oswald Mosely and his British Union of Fascists gained support from the general public and press, even filling the Royal Albert Hall. Jewish civilians were mistreated not only by the police, but also by other German individuals; whether they be loyal customers or just by-passers, anyone who dared to support or rebel was arrested and questioned. During this period, a wealthy German family, known as the Schmidt family, who were investors in support of the Nazi Party from its inception now question the ideals of Hitler and his one-party dictatorship. Jason and Emilia Schmidt and their two children, Matthew and Mia, live in Berlin where they reside in their exquisite mansion. Meanwhile, Emilia's parents, Romeo and Martha Schmidt, conveniently reside just opposite in a similarly-styled mansion. The family's support in helping Hitler rise within the government has been of benefit to them, but Matthew seems to have formed his own opinions on the matter.

Chapter 1

MY NAME IS MATTHEW Schmidt, well to be exact, my original name was Matthew Aarons, that was until my family became involved with the Nationalist Socialist German Workers' Party. I never understood why, but my grandfather and my mother saw something in Adolf Hitler that could probably change the culture in Germany and bring us back to glory. In their eyes, they saw financial and economic gain, in his eyes it was more than that, more than just politics. When I first met Hitler, on the occasion that he visited my house, there was a darkness in his eyes that no one dared notice, but I did. It was more than coldness; it was like something was troubling him. I did not realise what the issue was until he mentioned it without remorse at our dinner table. He thought that Germany was falling apart and President von Hindenburg was not focusing on the true cause of the matter. He explained that Germany was getting too soft and timid compared to the resisting countries, who had power in the Eastern countries. Germany was on a peddle stool that was about to crumble. I had to admit, he convinced them with his flowery sentences and hard-earned charisma, but it was when he mentioned the major issue that I almost stood up from my seat. His problem was the Jews. He blamed them for taking over most businesses in Germany, their expansion in communities, their impure blood and World War One. In his opinion, they were the cause of Germany's downfall and the result was our consequences – namely the Treaty of Versailles.

The reaction to his speech was priceless: my grandfather laughed and slapped him hard on the back agreeing with him but he argued that it was not all Jews but, only the ones that were "corrupt".

What the hell did he mean by that?

My father's fists were clenched and he eventually stormed out of the room, my mother sat there not knowing what to do but she forced a slight grin at Hitler. My grandmother was not present as she went to comfort my father, and my sister was bewildered by not just Adolf Hitler's comments but how the chaos was brewing in the house. After that dinner, I showed Adolf Hitler out to the door, after my mother and grandfather had a brief discussion about how they were going to support him financially and get him into power. As I opened the door to escort him out, he turned to me shaking my hand and asked me one simple question:

"Young man, how do you feel about the Jews?"

It threw me off at the time and all I did was shrug, trying to act like I did not hear his question. He smiled at me and laughed before instantly ruffling my hair, it was the only time I saw him smile, a genuine smile; I beamed at him and he waved at me as I closed the door. At the time, I did not see what the issue was, oh I knew he did not like Jews but from that smile I also knew he cared for this country and wanted to see it succeed, see Germany rise again. I did not know if he was born here, in Germany, since his accent was very rough compared to the average German spokesperson, but that did not matter. Maybe I could trust him. But when I stepped back into the dining room something in me turned and I had a feeling that something terrible was going to happen, no, much worse. And boy was I right. I was thirteen years old at the time, the year was 1930, and even though I was young, I already figured that my father wanted no association with Adolf Hitler. It made more sense as the years went by one by one, my father's original surname was Aarons; Aarons was a Jewish name that belonged to my grandfather who sadly passed away many years ago. My father practised the religious customs at a tender young age, he was born in Munich when my great grandparents moved to Germany many years ago. It wasn't until my parents married that he changed his surname to Schmidt because my mother's father was not a fan of his daughter taking on a Jewish name, yet he had nothing against my father.

My father taught us Judaism when my sister and I were old enough to understand what was right and what was wrong. Unlike him who was forced to learn about the religion, he gave us a choice if we wanted to or not, which we agreed we wanted because both of us were young and interested. My mother also learned some of the teachings, she did not believe in anything, however she got to understand through research about Jewish history and of course about the Bible later on. My mother never told my grandfather she was practising Judaism because she knew how much her father disliked religion; the only reason he even allowed my father to marry my mother was because my father had a large business that he owned in Germany which would help expand the Schmidt name.

At first, I was becoming interested in Judaism but my interest began to falter because other priorities came into my life such as sports, school and girls. Women around me always told me that I was an attractive boy. I was confronted by girls in school who would ask me out on dates but I declined most of the time because my studies were more important to me. I wanted to become two things in life and that was to work in any government and, if that did not work out, I wanted to get into the entertainment industry.

In my classes, I succeeded at only the subjects that intrigued me, particularly Drama, English, Maths, Science, and History. Outside of that, I was excellent in sports, especially hurdles and running distances; meanwhile, my father, who came home late from work most of the time, always gave me praise because the subjects I excelled in were essential in daily life. I was much closer to my father than my mother, but my mother was the main reason I wanted to go into politics because she was always teaching how if a man had the power to change laws, he had the power to change a country. That always stuck with me. So, when I met Adolf Hitler, a man who wanted to change the laws of the country to better the people and the lives of the communities I respected him for that even if he disliked Jewish people. However, after the constant arguments I saw between my father and mother about Hitler and his ideas, my thoughts on him began to slowly change.

My mother supported his ideals and so did my grandfather seeing as they were investing in him and his party; on the other hand, my father, who comes from Jewish ancestry disliked the abuse Hitler spat about the Jewish communities and Jews in general. It hurt him and because of that, in the year 1932, my mother wanted a divorce and so did my father. It broke my heart. It broke my sister's heart too. We did not know if it were really because of Adolf Hitler and the Nationalist Socialist German Workers' Party or because my father could not handle my mother being too deeply invested. The finalisation of the settlement of our house came under my mother, my father already had a house in Munich so he went to live there. But what brought us relief was that my sister and I were still able to visit him three times a week.

CHAPTER 2

THE DATE WAS 4TH JANUARY 1935, the new year had just passed and I was cycling on the new bike I had just bought for myself the previous Christmas. The weather was extremely cloudy, but from the forecast, there would be no rain today. I was making my way to my track session at my school; it was my last year before I would either head to university or decide to work with my mother later this year. My school was based in Berlin, not too far from my house; I attended a private school since my mother could afford it. Ever since Adolf Hitler became Fuhrer, the school system was never the same, especially for private schools. Some of my Jewish friends had already been expelled or told that they were no longer suitable to continue to the next year, it was stupid to me, but they were oblivious to the real reason behind their expulsion so they just accepted it.

Their parents did not complain, well, they did not have a choice too, and of course, in my school, most Jews have recently been kicked out too, some have been allowed to stay only because their parents willingly pleaded to pay double the amount for tuition fees and so forth. These were tough times and I had that feeling again that things were going to get much worse. My father, who has one of the biggest companies in Germany, was told to relocate to another area to continue his business, but of course, my father would never back down. Hitler decided to allow my father only because he knew us, and we were essentially the reason he was elevated to power in the government. My sister attends the same school as me and her uniform dress code did not change, neither did mine; however, there were some children who rolled into class wearing the famous swastika. I did not wear one, and neither did my sister, however I noticed my mother put a massive painting of one in the living room. She was accustomed to it and so was my grandfather. I however was not.

Once I arrived on the track, my coach saw me and waved like crazy in my direction, I sprinted towards him as fast I could, avoiding the muddy patches that were noticeable on the green grass. The weather was definitely chilly compared to a few hours before I left home, I stared at the grey clouds forming together like a herd in the sky: it was not dark but you could say it was still night-time if you were looking out your window. The time was only quarter to one and it felt like it was almost twelve, I shivered. It had not even snowed late last year, but I knew there was going to be snow around the corner very soon and I was not ready for it, not at all. Upon me arriving I saw two Nazi soldiers waltz inside the gate heading to my coach, we all paused our exercise routine and watched as one of the soldiers gripped roughly onto my coach's collar. One of my classmates named James Rogue who transferred here from another private school for misconduct confronted the second soldier trying to query him. I glanced at the others who all stood there turning their heads in fear, it was understandable, they did not want to get involved but whatever was going on was wrong. As soon as I turned back to face my coach, he was on the floor with blood running from his lip, the soldier's hand was formed into a fist and before I knew what was happening, he began beating him up without mercy. James was being held back by the other guard who I noticed was secretly smiling as if this were all part of their amusement, I could not take this any longer, even if I knew I would get into trouble. Running towards the first soldier I picked up one of the hurdles and whacked him right in the head with it without processing the consequences. All I heard was a loud crack and the guard fell right on the floor not moving. I backed away when I realised there was blood spreading from his hat.

Everything had happened so fast that I did not know how to react, I was only tired and annoyed with the mistreatment and the coach did not deserve to be beaten to a pulp. I was sitting outside my school office, with James next to me, he sat one seat away because I could tell he was afraid of me. Afraid of what I did. The soldier was pronounced dead, and his comrade who was also there on the track had tried to kill me for it, I would too if I were in his shoes. The door widened and the same guard who wanted to kill me walked out and caught me staring at him, we both glared at each other in disgust, he muttered some foul words under his breath and continued towards the exit. My headteacher ushered us in his office and James instantly got up and went inside, I trudged along behind him worried about what was going to happen to me.

Inside the room was my mother, the coach, and a man with slicked-back greasy hair with pale skin and a pointy nose structure; I knew he was important somehow. My mother did not bother to gaze at me but I already saw her expression when I entered the room: it was the face of disappointment, and I understood why she was; the man wearing the military-style uniform was eyeing my every move from the moment I came in till when I sat down. I felt like I had seen him before but I could not quite put my finger on it. Was he close to my mother, and if so, how close? My headteacher coughed to bring down the awkwardness in the room and commenced to speak:

"Well, I am glad that we are all sitting here in this room, I have about heard the incident that occurred a few hours ago and I believe there was indeed a misunderstanding. As you all know two soldiers who were on duty came to this school track to question Mr Fischer, the school's head coach, about why he and his fellow students were doing this when of course school is not open. The two soldiers were probably not informed that Mr Fischer has been doing this for years, which is odd to me, but they asked some questions and it got out of hand and one of them started hitting Mr Fischer for no reason. Then Mr Schmidt here hit the man with a metal hurdle to the head which sadly killed him, which is why we are all here today. So, what we need to do is come up with a solution and get everyone's opinion on the matter. Would you like to go first Mr Goebbels?"

So that was his name, that made more sense, I knew he was significant. So, it was Mr Joseph Goebbels. The famous politician and appointed Reich Minister of the media and press in Germany, he usually did public speaking around the country and was committed to his deep virulent views on anti-Semitism. I heard one of his speeches on the radio and then turned it off. Not only was he like Hitler, he was trying to take after him, which was complete nonsense; a man who visited my house a couple of times but I never took notice of till now, which is not my fault at all. If there was one thing I always felt whenever I was around him was a deep hatred for him and the other politicians in that party including Adolf Hitler: I grew to hate them all after what my father told me they tried to do to him. All because he was of Jewish ancestry. It made me sick. They really hated Jewish people that much, and for what? To satisfy themselves so they can distinguish that they are not the same, we were all still human beings, but I knew common sense like that was never discussed in their regular meetings. Goebbels took his eyes off me and ran his hands through his hair before answering my headmaster's question.

"Well, to be quite honest with you all, those two soldiers were new to the SS, they were probably not informed which I will discuss next time with Himmler about. Now, my guess is that we will brush this incident behind us and forget that it even happened, Mr Fischer will receive some money from me for the misconduct he received today since it was unacceptable. And that is all I have to say. But I have to say, young man, the way you killed that soldier was definitely on point, it was like you knew where to strike him to make sure he was static. Have you killed a person before?"

My head was down and a finger tapped me, it was James, I raised my head up instantly and looked Goebbels in the face, he was not smiling at me but in his eyes, there was something that glimmered signalling to me that he was impressed. I did not know what he wanted me to say, but I could not be disrespectful, I mean I did not want to die; I had a life I wanted to live.

"No sir, this is my first time killing someone, I have never murdered anyone before."

"I see, you would be useful in the SS if you joined when you grow older, people of your calibre with strength like that deserve to be assigned to jobs to handle issues the SS are consistently protecting. Well of course it is your choice, is there a purpose you have found in your life you want to achieve?"

"Yes sir, I want to be either in the government or work in the entertainment business."

"Entertainment business? Ha, exceptionally good choice of words, the arts have always been taken for granted, it makes me sick, but as head of all of that in this country, when you are confident to talk about this in person. Your mother can contact me anytime when you are ready."

"Thank you, sir, I really do appreciate it."

Nodding at me, he stood up and made his way out the door, signalling my coach, Mr Fischer to follow him; Mr Fischer rose instantly and left the room shutting the door loudly. From what I could see I stared at my mother who also stood up from her chair and grabbed my arm, her nails digging into my flesh, she bowed and offered her apologies for my reckless behaviour and swung open the door while dragging me with her. James gazed at me with a worried expression, he knew that even though this whole murder scene was going to be swept under the rug, in his mind it could not be erased. And he was right, I still remembered every detail, and it haunted me for the rest of my life. All I wanted to know was why James and I or the rest of the students present were not kicked out of our school, and then I remembered something, my mother was especially important in the political world in Germany which meant she brought Goebbels here to save me from getting expelled. Convinced my headmaster that if he tried to kick me out, he would probably die, and for my trouble, he asked me what I wanted to do because he knew now, I owed him.

CHAPTER 3

"I HEARD WHAT HAPPENED to you from mother, did you murder a Nazi soldier?"

AGAIN, AND AGAIN WITH this nonsense. My sister knew how to infuriate me at my worst, I purposely ignored the question and trudged to the living room to turn on the radio. I adjusted the set to one of my favourite shows, Amos 'n' Andy, it always came on in the evenings. I relaxed on the chair and listened to what they were saying, blocking out the rest of what was going on around me. That was until I heard my sister calling my name over and over, and over and over again, I could not take it anymore, everyone was trying to annoy me today. Rising from the chair, I went to her and told her bluntly to leave me alone, she giggled at me which further pushed my buttons, she was not taking me seriously. All of a sudden, the doorbell rang, and we both froze. We waited for our maid, Beatrice to answer. The doorbell rang again, it seemed urgent. I tiptoed to the entrance area and searched around to see who was present, there was no Beatrice, which meant I had to answer. Mother was at work, and I was suspended from school, and Mia was not going because she was apparently "ill"; she was such an amazing liar. Unlocking the door, my eyes widened and right in front of me was Joseph Goebbels, why was he here? He was wearing a much more casual fit compared to when I last saw him, and he was carrying a packaged envelope in a brown casing, in the middle was the swastika sign.

"Ah, young man, we meet again, is your mother at home?"

"No sir, she is at work, she usually comes home late. What is that you have there?"

"These are some mere documents for her regarding some political issues the party is having right now, the Fuhrer decided to fill her in on some of them."

"Is that all you wanted sir?"

"Young man, if you were a part of the party, I would love to tell you but you are not, so I will just send one of my soldiers to give it to her tomorrow."

"That would be no problem, sir, you can leave me with the documents and I can give them to her when she arrives."

"No, no, that would be unwise, I will do as I insisted, you do not need to worry."

"But...."

"I insist Matthew Schmidt. Please do not argue with me."

I most certainly did not want to get on his bad side, his tone had changed dramatically, a more sinister aura was becoming visible, and I was not going to challenge him, there was no point. Shaking my hand, he went down our stone steps and then turned back to me and asked me, "Young man, how is your father doing?" I did not know his intentions behind those words but it made me nervous, I did my casual shrug and he nodded at me before strolling off down the pavement.

Why would he ask me that? Was my father causing them trouble?

My stomach twisted and the rush of nausea came strongly through my system, I did not want to think the worst but it stuck to the back of my mind. If they ever harmed my father, I would personally kill them all, including Goebbels himself. I resumed my seat in the living room and processed the conversation I just had, the horrible feeling I had all those years ago was haunting me again, the discussion reminded me of the situation I had with Hitler back in 1930. I did not know if he was influenced by that man but Goebbels gave me the same energy, he was polite yet dangerous, it was like he was wearing a mask, as if his true nature was being concealed and this act was his solace. The peace within that was containing a monster that was ready to explode, my eyes widened, just like me, what I had done to the soldier three days ago was the real me. That was how I felt about all of them. The smiling, the greetings, even my dialect was all an act to contain that anger, the pain, the agony I was feeling everyday living in this imprisoned country. That was the real me, just like Goebbels, just like Hitler, I had something within my soul that was dark and evil, the only difference between me and them was that they were better at disguising it.

My reasons for my actions had been taken to not only the school but to a private court session in Munich involving James, an unknown woman, my mother and Mr Fischer. We spent at least two and half hours in there and my mind was bogged down, the questions I was getting were not only pressuring me but making me more fearful of saying words that did not match up with my other sentences. Currently,

I was taking a break with James outside the main room, we were sitting on a bench biting deep into our sandwiches which consisted of ham, lettuce and cheese. They had been made by my mother who willingly decided to tag along just to see if I would say a story out of context. Mr Fischer was sitting to the far left on another bench, I gazed at him wondering what was going through his mind since during the sessions he was so quiet and tranquil that the woman was nervous herself. She had hesitated in throwing insults at him because his mood gave her chills. As I was staring at him, his posture instantly straightened and he caught my gaze, I tried whipping my head away and pretending I was still eating but he smiled and came in our direction. Once he was a few metres away from us, he signalled a finger at James, and to my stupefaction, he abruptly sprinted towards the man. My heart almost jumped out of my mouth, no wonder I dropped my sandwich so quickly, he must have done that to scare me on purpose. Sometimes I questioned why I hung around him more often than I did my sister.

Things were not going as my mother and I expected during the third session of the court meeting, it all started when James started to speak again, it was his change in his story that alerted me and I was not having it. After consistently telling the woman that he interfered before I got the hurdle and whacked the soldier in the back of his skull, he now was mentioning that he had actually tried to stop me from doing the murderous act but I ignored him and went and hit the soldier anyway. It not only angered me, but made me question if we were really friends or not, I had to restrain myself from getting out of my seat and hitting his face like a punching bag because it would not only make me look like the villain but it would also prove the point he made earlier.

Throughout that last meeting, I glared at this fool purposefully waiting for him to even just turn his eyes on me but he did not, he knew what he was spouting was full of lies, he kept fidgeting in his chair nervously and trying to straighten his collar by loosening the buttons to relax. Well, it was not working because he began asking the woman if he was allowed to be excused to go to the toilet almost five times and I knew it was not for an actual toilet break; he was regretting everything he said. The woman came to an overall conclusion that there would be no charges against me but I already knew that was the case, my mother had informed me that the woman had already been paid a large sum of money before the meeting even took place by none other than the man himself, Joseph Goebbels, which meant that whatever James had been planning failed miserably. After the meeting, I confronted him about the trash talk he had been spewing to the woman, he denied it and said he was paid to say it by Mr Fischer. It did make sense to me why James had left with him, but why would Mr Fischer want me to go to prison?

Something was not adding up.

Ordering him to showcase the money, he pulled out 1,000 RM and placed it in my hand; I instantly tore it into four pieces throwing it on the floor before stampeding and shuffling it under my shoe. A petrified James backed away from me and tears ran down his face, I glared at him in disgust. What annoyed me was not that he tried to set me up but that he did not bother reporting to me that he was going to do it, he made me sick. The absolute nerve of this fool, he was lucky that I did not have a metal hurdle on me right now because he would have surely been next on my list.

The car waiting for my mother and I was a VW Series 3 convertible prototype, our driver was my mother's long-time friend Bryson Bird, he was an unusual man but he was a very trustworthy associate, my mother had known him since they were teenagers. As he widened the back door for me, he placed something in my mother's hand, who was in front of me, with ease and gave her a troubled expression. From the communication with his eyes, my mother's eyes darkened and she told me that she had matters to attend to; I was so confused by this change of plan that I tried querying with her about what she was so desperately hiding. Without answering me, she gave me a comforting look and rubbed my cheeks reassuring me that everything was okay. I doubted it. There were some issues that she had to take care of and I felt like I was in her way, no, Mia and I were in her way, my mother had not been the same person after the split with my father, it was as if she had forgotten that man even existed, to begin with. Her schedules have resulted in her coming home past 11:00 pm. She no longer paid attention to Mia or even me as much as we expected, it was challenging, I got it, but there was no way Mia would understand at all. I mean, the girl was turning seventeen in August, she was still a child, and so was I, but my mother never saw children as most parents would usually do, she saw us as fully grown individuals. It made sense to me. In the past I had to take care of Mia while my mother came home late. Whether it was assisting Beatrice with cooking dinner to taking Mia home from school, my little sister was my responsibility. I fully understood why she did not react a certain way when I ripped up James' money. I was growing up and not allowing people to treat me otherwise, and my mother respected that about her son. My only concern was those documents that she finally received from Goebbels the other night, he had sent a soldier the other day like he promised to physically hand it to her when my mother was free, and oh was he on time. I was in the living room listening to the radio when Beatrice had gracefully taken it from the soldier who randomly saluted at her and shouted, "Hail Fuhrer!!", it was weird why all the soldiers did that however we had to do it as well in classes. All I wanted to know was what information my mother was receiving that was so vital. I needed to know.

CHAPTER 4

TODAY IS SEPTEMBER 3rd, 1935; it has almost been over eight months since my case, and life has not been getting better or shall I say going as smoothly as I wanted it to. Eight months back, Joseph Goebbels had sent my mother a document about something incredibly significant that I was very intrigued about.

What happened?

Well, I will explain it to you since I have time; let me take it back to February 10th, 1935. My mother was of course coming home late which was not surprising to me or my sister. Beatrice had decided to fill in for her since my mother had promised to double her pay. Seemed to my recollection on the day before, she had to see Adolf Hitler because of some "major" concerns on the new policies the Nazi Party had been deciding to put out for the country. I did not believe a word that came from her lips even though my sister and Beatrice nodded their heads like obedient dogs both wagging their tails as if my mother was going to serve them a nice treat. It was pathetic. But then I realised that this would be the only chance I would get because not only was she not coming home tonight, she was coming home the next day which meant I had plenty of time. All I needed to know was where she hid the keys to her cupboards and drawers, and the only person who usually was allowed access in her room when she was gone was Beatrice so there was a possibility that Beatrice had a clue where it was. As soon as my mother left the house, around 4:00 pm, I headed straight to the window to carefully watch her get escorted into her car by Bryson, he looked up at the window without any hesitation like a hawk. I had already closed the curtains suspecting that to occur, he had always been very unusual to me but at the same time, I had that slight feeling he was a smart fellow as well. The problem was I would never know because I was never going to ask.

Two hours had passed since my mother left, and Beatrice had not arrived yet, I tried calling her number on our telephone set but there was no answer. This made me even more suspicious yet frightened because I had a plan already on the go yet Beatrice was the number one instrument for that plan to succeed, and that was essential. Bolting to Mia's room, I slammed the door wide almost knocking over her small wooden table positioned next to it, she jumped up and fell off her bed hitting her elbow on the carpet floor roughly. Mia rubbed both her knees and scurried towards me with viciousness in her eyes before I knew what was happening. I felt my face start to sting as if I had been slapped. Well, I did get slapped, however, it felt much more intentional than I expected. I rubbed my cheek bewildered by her sudden anger. From the dark presence surrounding her, I knew that I had either interrupted something important or there was something she knew that I was involved in. It was too soon for fighting but it was clear she did not have the same mindset I had. I anticipated her right hand coming at my face once again, I grabbed it lightly staring at Mia in her face indicating that it was pointless, she dropped her hand and trudged back to her bed and sat in silence. I went to sit on her wooden chair near the corner of her room adjusting my neck sideways thinking about what was going on.

"Mia, I have a question to ask you, if you do not mind."

"I do not want to talk to you right now Matthew I am not in the mood."

"Listen, this is particularly important, where is Beatrice? I thought she was supposed to be here by 5:15 pm."

"Well, that is the issue, she is in the hospital right now, she got into an accident."

"Accident? Wait, so she is not coming today? Not even after?"

"Are you crazy Matthew? The poor woman almost died in a car crash this evening on her way here and you blabbering about if she can still make it here?"

"I...I did not mean it like that...wait...how long did you know about this?"

"Just received the information thirty minutes ago from mother through the telephone, she has decided that you are in charge of the house until she comes back tomorrow. But that is not the point...Beatrice could have.... could have died."

"Understandable, so...what about......you know...."

"What?"

"Do you know where mother keeps her keys because I know Beatrice is the only one who knows..."

A LOST SOUL: THE REVELATION

"Her keys to her room? The keys are downstairs in her drawer opposite the cupboard on the third column. Why do you even want her keys?"

"Well.... I erm.... there was something mother told me to get in her room yesterday and I forgot to give it to her so...yeah."

"Weird. Mother would have reported this to all of us yesterday, are you sure?"

"Yes, and how do you even know where mother's keys are at?"

"Just saw Beatrice put her keys there one time so I suspected that it must be where mother hides them, it is no big deal. And stop changing the question, I am going to call mother to confirm if what you are saying is true or not."

"No!! No, no, no, and no, you need to trust me, she did, she discussed it with me in private before I went to bed yesterday, but thanks anyway. Just promise me you will not call her, and she is busy, remember? Just promise me."

"I promise okay, I will not call her."

I went to give her a bear hug, but she hesitated and drew away from me like a wounded animal, I did not know what to say, I mean she was hurting because Beatrice got into a car accident on her way here. Shaking my head, I saluted her, quietly shut the door and made my way as quickly as I could down the stairs. Heading towards the cupboard, I scanned the third section and lifted the pile of clean shiny books that were all aligned in one line on the side of the shelf. Removing them all at once with both hands, I noticed a bright golden object flat on the surface on top of one of her paper sheets. Taking off the sheets, I put my hand in the middle and drew out the object while warily checking around to see if anyone was watching me. I sighed with relief and kissed the key on my lips, it tasted horrible but it was worth it, now all I had to do was find what was in the documents. This was a chance that I was never going to get back and I was not going to waste that opportunity.

Creeping up the stairs without disturbing my sister, I tiptoed like an assassin ready to kill his target at the door. Turning the key to the right, I slowly pushed the door open and stuck my head inside her room. I noticed the drawers in the distance. There it was, right there, opposite her mirror wall, I stepped inside feeling guilty for intruding and shut the door as quietly as I could. My mother's room was always tidy so when it came to Beatrice being allowed to organise from her clothes to dusting her floors, Beatrice knew how to make her job easier for her whenever she got her pay rise. I stared at the massive mirror and examined myself, it was like I was gaping deep into my soul, what was that scripture in the Bible it said? "For what profits a man if he gains the whole world but loses his soul?" For some odd reason chills went down my spine when I recalled that verse in my mind, I stared at the drawer not knowing what was inside, what I was gaining if I opened that drawer, it is not like I was doing anything illegal. I lived in this house too, I had a right to know what type of things my mother was doing, but then again, I was invading her privacy without her even knowing. Shaking my head, I went and pulled the drawer worried that the document would not be inside. My eyes brightened, a small smile curled on my lips, I was wrong, it was right here, the brown casing, the document was in front of me.

A LOST SOUL: THE REVELATION

It was right there, and literally within my grasp, I felt so excited and overjoyed, now I had the chance to find what treasure was being concealed in the envelope. I stared at the time, it was almost seven, I had plenty of time; however, I did not want to waste reading it, all I wanted was a clear idea of what was going on, it would take away that weight that had been on my shoulders these past few weeks. I slipped it out of the drawer and opened the flap, it seems like the envelope was already opened by my mother, which made things much more straightforward. I took out a five-page document which was exceptionally light in my hand, that was odd, was the casing Goebbels was carrying just a stunt? I shrugged my shoulders and knelt down near my mother's bed while placing the document on the bedsheet. The bold black ink title caught my attention. It said "Confidential Policy: Nuremberg Laws".

What was the Nuremberg Laws?

I flipped over to the next page and my eyes widened in horror, I shook my head and started again just to check if I was dreaming. There was a large paragraph indicating the explanation of the policy and on the side was the list of politicians within the party who contributed to the policy ideas. And I noticed a familiar name on the top.

Adolf Hitler.

I scrunched my fists. This was not acceptable, no, this was no policy, this was just hatred towards fellow Jewish communities and an escalation of anti-Semitism. It read:

"The Nuremberg Laws is an ideal policy that has been decided by the German Reich to be evaluated and later on pronounced as a new law in the home of our German people. One, the Reichsbürgergesetz (German: "Law of the Reich

Citizen"), deprived Jews of German citizenship, designating them "subjects of the state." The other, the Gesetz zum Schutze des Deutschen Blutes und der Deutschen Ehre ("Law for the Protection of German Blood and German Honour"), usually called simply the Blutschutzgesetz ("Blood Protection Law"), forbade marriage or sexual relations between Jews and "citizens of German or kindred blood."

I could not read anymore, it was too much for me to comprehend, I closed the document and slipped it roughly back into the envelope sickened and revolted by what I had just indulged my pure eyes into.

CHAPTER 5

AFTER WHAT I HAD EXAMINED from that document, I questioned what the Nazi Party were really up to. At the bottom of the first page, they would decree the act – they had chosen the 15th of September, the policy would become apparent on the 15th of September. Now that you have a clear idea of what the Nuremberg Laws are, I can fast forward to where I am currently.

Like I informed you all, it is the 3rd of September 1935, the policy will be authorised in 12 days. Am I ready for this? No. Have I told anyone or questioned my mother why she is involved in such a scandalous scheme? No. How can I? There will be no solution if I argue with her, this is her job, she is invested in a monster that is wreaking havoc in the Jewish community all because their blood is impure. What a foolish joke. On the other hand, I have informed one particular person about this, my father, Jason Aarons, he had a right to know. The only trouble was when I told him his reaction was not completely what I expected, he appeared tired physically and mentally as if he had given up on life, I felt so emotional and heartbroken. Not just him but other Jews were getting harassed, misused, and treated harshly by even other non-Jewish Germans which was sickening and horrible. Once I explained it to my father all he did was pat me on the shoulder and he specifically said, "Matthew, my dear boy, first of all, you should have never gone into your mother's room without her permission and taken her key, that is stealing. Secondly, I was expecting a policy like this, I am not wowed or dazzled by what you have informed me because deep down I suspected something like this was coming, maybe not as serious as what you have said but something along those lines. All we have to do is stand strong, go through the tough and thin and remain steadfast because the God of Abraham, Isaac and Jacob will protect us." I nodded in agreement at his response, but deep down, I knew he was in denial, who was going to save us? God? This was not Moses and the Israelites fleeing from Pharaoh, this was Hitler we were discussing, he was no Pharaoh, he was a devil, he was much worse.

My mind was warning me that Germany's culture was being redesigned by this dictatorship that Hitler and his party held so onto so dearly, it made me question if I wanted to be part of the government in this country at all, any government in that case, why did Hitler not understand that his ideology was flawed? Jewish people had been living here for years and years, that is what I was taught in my history lessons, that was what my father told me, and yet the Nazis still saw Jews as parasites who had taken over its host, Germany. Even when I cycled in the lonesome streets, all I saw was consternation and terror in the people, the SS police were everywhere, storming the streets and corners checking and searching for targets that were out of place; it frightened me. If there really was a God up there in the clouds like my father kept believing in, where was he in this day and age? Did he abandon his chosen people? I did not know anything, my belief in the Jewish teachings had disappeared a long time ago, once Hitler came into power in 1933 that was when I knew there was no hope. And now that I see the children, old women and men huddled up together in the cold, trying to warm themselves up outside the slums in Berlin, my motivation for a saviour to rescue them was over. We needed to act upon ourselves, the only question was who was capable of leading? The law did state that anyone who opposed the Nazis through the negative press or public speaking were thrown into jail, or maybe secretly killed. That was just a theory.

"Hey young man, watch where you are going!"

I snapped back into reality and swerved my bicycle left to avoid a passing dog that was crouched on the road, I crashed into a garbage bin knocking myself harshly against the brick wall. I thought I heard my backbone crack, maybe it was just my imagination, I groaned whilst lifting a banana peel off my blonde curly hair, it was covered in ants crawling over the bottom layer. Bemused by the display, I threw the peel out onto the pavement but I did not notice two layered muddy black boots standing right there in front of me. Hesitantly gazing up at the anonymous figure I realised it was an SS trooper, I brushed myself and headed for my bicycle which was still lying there flat-first on the side of the road. Once I tried to get on, the man grabbed my clothing and pulled me back forcefully almost making me stumble to the floor. My anger was starting to rise again and I did not want to start a fight with a Nazi soldier, the last time that happened it did not turn out well.

"Is there something I can do for you, sir?"

"Did you not see the dog out on the road young man?"

"No sir, I did not see the dog, I was..."

"You were in your little world. You almost killed it."

"But sir I didn't even touch it, can I please get to where I am going, I have to head back home."

"Sorry but you have to come with me, not only are you not admitting to your faults but you are not supposed to be around these parts. Are you a Jewish citizen?""

"No, but I was coming back from seeing someone in Munich and this was the only avenue that was accessible."

"No excuses young man, I need you to come with me, and you did not answer my question, are you a Jewish Citizen?"

"I do not think you should be touching my bike; my mother is Emilia Schmidt; she is very close to the Fuhrer so you should be careful sir."

"I.... I did not know....my apologies Mr Schmidt, I thought you were just a by-passer, just make sure you do not come around these parts again, understood?"

"You have my word sir; I will find another route next time."

"Good, let us keep this little incident between us, have a nice journey back home."

Climbing back on my bicycle, I started to cycle away from him not knowing that he was still staring at me, I could feel his eyes piercing through my flesh. Sweat trickled down my forehead, this man must have known I was from the Schmidt family, my mother was famous in Germany, but what if he did not know I was her son? There were many children in Germany who had blonde hair like mine, my problem was there weren't many wealthy individuals who dressed like me, so what was the issue? Was it my father? The thoughts of the policies I had scanned all those months ago were still toying in my mind, I had to get my father away from here, he had to leave Germany, he had no choice. All that was possible was The Deutsche Reichsbahn, also known as the German National Railway, the German State Railway, German Reich Railway, and the German Imperial Railway, was the German national railway system created after the end of World War I from the regional railways of the individual states of the German Empire. From what I knew thanks to my history classes. If that was not possible, my father had to just wait, and handle whatever issues he was having with the SS, it would be for the best. I swerved my bicycle down the main street and parked it beside the stairs when I reached my house. It was at that point that I caught something out of the corner of my eye appearing right there alongside the pavement. Two soldiers were marching towards me at an average speed, once they saw me, one of them asked if I was the son of Emilia Schmidt, to which I nodded in agreement. They both eyed each other, and the second soldier put his hand deep into his waistcoat, my heart was thumping faster and faster, I did not know what he was about to do but his demeanour shook me to the core. Getting ready to fight back, his hand revealed a book which he handed to me politely, I relaxed and grabbed it from him wondering what it was. The other man informed me it was from Goebbels, a recommendation from the Fuhrer himself, I bowed gracefully and they went on their way down the other side of the road.

As I slammed the door, a head popped out and I realised that it was my sister, Mia. The facial expression she displayed was a mixture of happiness and humour, something splendid must have happened for her to be joyous for no reason. Making her way enthusiastically down the stairs, she launched herself at me like a predator pouncing on its prey; what the hell was her problem? Mia giggled and grabbed my hand yanking me to the living room, I was not amused by her antics but I went along with it, she seated me on the sofa like a misbehaved child who is about to be lectured by his parents. I waited patiently for the words to pour out her mouth but nothing came out, it was like she did not want to tell me but at the same time wanted to tell me, I was more confused than she was, and then she began to speak:

"Matthew you will not believe this but guess what happened in class today?"

"Well to be honest with you I do not know, so I guess you are going to tell me."

"Correct! From what our teachers have informed us, our country is going to host the Olympics next year! Is that not great?"

"Well....to be completely honest with you I don't care about those kinds of things anymore."

"But I thought you loved the Olympics? Do you not love track anymore?"

"Yes and no, is that all you wanted to tell me?"

"Pretty much."

"Well, this was a pointless conversation, I have work to submit tomorrow, and you wasted ten valuable minutes of my time just to spurt out that Germany is hosting the Olympics next year."

"What is wrong with you? Did you get into trouble again? And what is that book you are holding; can I see it?"

"No. Leave me be, and please next time you want to give me news make sure it is important."

I rose from the sofa and strutted up the stairs leaving a confused Mia still sitting down on the chair; I could not blame her, the Olympics were pretty much essential to Germany, well for every country worldwide, the reason I did not care as much was that I had no idea how the Fuhrer was planning to portray the German nation. What was undeniable was that any Jewish athletes around the world participating in the Olympics were going to be in a heap of trouble and mess because I knew the Swastika was going to be present everywhere in the stadium. And I was not going to entertain that, not for my sister, my mother, my father or even Hitler himself.

CHAPTER 6

WAIT A MINUTE. THIS book seems so familiar. I saw it in my mother's workroom many years ago but I never considered it. As soon as I examined the book properly, I read the bold title out loud, "Mein Kampf" which meant "My Fight", the author was none other than Adolf Hitler. I did not realise he had written a book, was it recently? I checked the back cover and then opened the first few pages, it said published on 18th July 1925, which was way over ten years ago. I threw the book on my bed deciding not to indulge myself in it, but then something in me was curious to discover what the man had to say, what his views were ten years ago and had it evolved or changed. I wanted to know where this all stemmed from and I wanted to know his goal, what did he want for this country? What did he want to bring to Germany? All these thoughts flowed like water into my mind, and I could not help but pick up the book, lock my door, and start reading; my assignments had to wait.

The book was 720 pages, an awfully long book, but the more I read, the more I began to understand why he thought the way he did, why he acted the way he did, his ideals, his plans against the Treaty of Versailles, leading Germany on top once again, these were all coming from a man who was passionate about a country he fought to protect since the First World War. His work's description of the process by which he became antisemitic and outlines his political ideology and plans for Germany made sense to me but I did not agree that some of the reasons he stated were good enough points to support his hatred towards the Jews. Not only did I find this section offensive towards my family from my father's side, but I was also stricken by his racist ideology, identifying the Aryan as the "genius" race and the Jew as the "parasite," and declaring the need for Germans to seek living space (Lebensraum) in the East at the expense of the Slavs and the hated Marxists of Russia. Moreover, his anger against the results of the First World War calls into consideration his revenge strategies against France. Once I was halfway through the novel, something stuck out to me that made me have to examine it twice, according to Hitler, it was "the sacred mission of the German people to assemble and preserve the most valuable racial elements, and raise them to the dominant position." In addition, he says "All who are not of a good race are chaff," which made me question the sole purpose of his ideal race because not everyone was supposed to be the same. It was necessary for Germans to "occupy themselves not merely with the breeding of dogs, horses, and cats but also with care for the purity of their blood." Hitler ascribed international significance to the elimination of Jews, which "must necessarily be a bloody process," he wrote. The words, phrases kept me thinking, even when Beatrice knocked on my door, I was too fixed on the novel, it was addictive.

The time was 11:00 pm, I had been reading the book nonstop in my room for almost six or seven hours, my mind was bogged down, my brain was embedded with quotes, I had delved so deep that I was drowning in the ink. I heard a large knock on my door, this time it did not feel like a welcoming knock, I got up from my bed and unlocked the door and there standing in front of me was my mother. She did not look pleased with me, I could easily tell, she was not the type to frown ever, yet when she did it meant two things: you got in trouble in school or you did something that she eventually discovered. Well, I was not in trouble for school so I played out the second option, I wonder what I did wrong. Storming into my room, she slammed the door, and ordered me to sit on my chair, I mean I was a young adult but it felt like I was being treated like a child again, she leaned against my front door examining me up and down without a care in the world. I was twitching my thumbs because I was anxious about what was about to happen, I felt cornered like a rat in a mousetrap about to die, I was mentally dying inside and the way my mother was glaring at me was not comforting either.

"Matthew, I want you to tell me the truth and nothing but the truth, do you hear me?"

"Yes mother, I promise to tell you the truth. But may I ask what this is all about?"

"Your sister told me that you have been acting vastly different for the past few months, and I have been noticing it too recently. She said that she told you about the Olympics but you were not pleased. Is there a reason why?"

"Well, I was busy and she told me at the wrong time, and I...I did not think it was important."

"Well for your correction, it is, the Fuhrer will be making a statement there, and you must be enthusiastic about it because I will be sitting with them once that day arrives."

"Is that all mother?"

"No, Mia told me that you started to act different since you asked about my keys back when Beatrice had a car accident."

"I do not know what Mia is talking about, I never asked her about any keys."

"Really? Mia confessed to me that you wanted to check something in my room because I told you so the day before. Am I wrong Matthew?"

"Mother I can explain...."

"No, you cannot explain, I want to know what you went in my room for, your sister is already in trouble and so will you if you are not careful."

"I...I was.... I took a document from your drawer."

"The one that Mr Goebbels had sent to me? Now did you read it?"

"I.... I......I do not know what you mean..."

"ANSWER ME, CHILD! DID YOU READ WHAT WAS INSIDE?"

"Yes mother, I did."

I raised my head to explain but she was not listening, there was something I saw in her eyes that almost caused me to curl up in a ball, I wanted to cry but I could not, she struck my face, her nails scratching on my skin; it was unexpected and painful. My mother started to scream at me, yelling at me words I had never expected her to say, but I was hardly listening to her, I knew she was hurting. I just did not know how much. Instead of staying there to listen, I grabbed the book on my bed, pushed her out the way and headed down the stairs making my way to the front door.

"WHERE DO YOU THINK YOU ARE GOING CHILD?! COME BACK HERE THIS INSTANT!"

Whipping my head around to face her, I did something that never in my life I would have envisioned doing, I spoke a word that I knew was blasphemous to any woman, let alone my own mother. My anger consumed me and I shouted, "Go to hell you Hündin!" and I said it with extreme passion. The whole house went silent, Beatrice appeared from the living room dropping her cleaning brush, my sister who was also downstairs stared at me not knowing what to say or do, and my mother, who was halfway down the staircase, did not know how to respond. I did not know what to do either. All I could do was stare at the three women in my house, I did not feel guilty, or ashamed, just an overwhelming feel of relief that I finally spoke how I truly felt. And it felt terrific.

Unlocking the front door, I closed it and ran towards my bicycle which was still parked along the stone steps, got on and stared back at the door waiting for my mother to come outside to stop me. But the bolts did not unlock nor did I hear the shouting of my name. I waited for a while weighing out my options, was what I said really worth it? Well, I did not care even if they did. Figuring out where to head to, a bulb popped into my brain, it was the only destination I had, I had to go and see my father, he would allow me to stay with him for a while. Turning back to the house I used to view as a comforting home, I held tightly to the book I had, and tucked it inside my jacket before setting off down the abandoned streets surrounded by the gloomy night sky.

CHAPTER 7

UPON ARRIVING SAFELY at my father's home, I noticed the change in house structure as I approached it, but it did not make much sense to me, I knew, however, that it did not seem the same as before. Five soldiers were standing out the gate once I arrived at the entrance, it was not just them, some civilians were huddling outside the gate too. What was happening? Pushing my way through, I confronted one of the soldiers and questioned him about what was going on, he stared at me and purposely ignored my question, this increased my fury even further. I instantly grabbed his clothing and tried to get his attention, he suddenly backhanded me in my mouth. Some of the people backed away worried about what was about to happen, I touched my lip and glared at the crimson liquid on my thumb, I wiped it off and raised my fists ready to fight. The man smiled grotesquely at me and showcased a pistol he had hidden in his inner pocket, but I did not care, the standoff lasted until a soldier I recognised came in between and held us back from escalating by coming between us and holding us apart. It was the soldier that had stopped me back at the slums when I was heading back home the day before, he whispered some words into the aggressive soldier's ear and then saluted and marched off to a second area of the house. The crowd were wooed by the display and tried to get close to me, the soldier revealed his weapon in a warning that not a finger was to be laid on me, he whipped his head around to face me and smiled.

"Sorry for all of that drama Mr Schmidt, but what are you doing here?"

"I came to see my father, Jason Aarons, he lives in this house. Why is there a crowd of people around here?"

"Does your mother know that you are here?"

"No, and she has no right to know, I don't even want to discuss about that woman."

"I apologise for not introducing myself to you before, my name is Franz Abromeit."

"Sir, what happened in my father's house?"

The man put his head down slowly before grabbing my shoulder. I stared at him confused but then I noticed there were tears rolling down his face.

Why was he crying?

Mr Abromeit led me around to the back of the gate avoiding the large crowd gathering on the high street. I turned my face back to him but the tears were gone.

Did he know my father? I had never heard of him. Nor has my father ever mentioned about Mr Abromeit.

Once we reached my father's back garden, I ordered him to release me and he immediately let go of my arm. Mr Abromeit gazed into my eyes before grabbing my shoulders again. He began to ramble but I could not begin to understand the words flowing out his mouth. Whatever had happened, it had scarred him. Or worse. I closed my eyes before asking Mr Abromeit to get to the point. His mouth shut instantly.

What was his problem?

I was getting annoyed with his antics.

"Sir, can you please tell me what occurred in my father's house?"

He loosened his grip on my shoulders and whispered some words in my ear. My eyes widened and I pushed him roughly away from me. Mr Abromeit understood my frustration.

What was I saying? He did not understand anything.

My anger rose and I tackled him to the ground. He fell hitting his head on the grass, and tried to shield himself. But I was not done with him. My hands were ready to cause damage, and I was not going to stop hitting him till I was satisfied. The more I punched him, whether it was his stomach, head, face or even his legs, the more Mr Abromeit screamed. Something in me warned me to stop but I pushed it aside and kept punching his face. And then I stopped. I don't know why. Maybe it was because my hands were bloody. No. It was something else. It didn't matter anyways. I rose from the grass and watched the man in front of me rise from the floor looking at me with tears in his eyes. And then I noticed his mouth was about to open. I didn't want to hear anything from this man yet I listened.

"I......I am so sorry that you had to hear this from me, but......."

"I don't care what you have to say. You have said enough. All I want to know is who killed him?!"

My body was shaking tremendously. The more I stood here, in my father's back garden.

My father......

I did not realise the tears rolling down to my soft rosy cheeks. I had just talked to him yesterday and I had come here to see him. But that would never happen. I would never get to see his face again. Mr Abromeit patted my shoulder trying to comfort me but stopped when he saw my fists curl up again.

My father was dead. Dead. I shivered. The word gave me chills.

After I had calmed down, Mr Abromeit and I headed back to the front of the house. But we had not been walking in silence. No. He had decided to explain to me the information he had received from his superiors about the tragic accident.

"Sir, how does that even make any sense? My father would never commit suicide!"

"Matthew, I understand it is difficult for you to digest, but as his son you have a right to see his body if you desire, I suggest you should not but it is your choice."

"I want to see it."

I wanted to see it, no, I wanted to just see my father, there was no way in hell he killed himself, it could not be true. It was all a lie. I knew it was. My father would never kill himself, that went against everything he stood for, it went against his religion, it went against what he taught me. Mr Abromeit cleared the gate passageway shooting his pistol in the air twice for the civilians to move on, they obediently parted like the Red Sea and we both walked through it as if we were deities. The soldiers in front of us saw Mr Abromeit and saluted showing us the front door, he signalled his guards to handle the people at the gate and to not let them in, he made a sign and I knew what it meant.

Kill anyone who gets in the way.

I had seen Goebbels do that sign when we were back in the school office, not only were these people powerful but they had no sympathy for their German people, whatever needed to be handled was handled. Pushing open the front door, he escorted me upstairs where there were more soldiers outside a particular door, I recognised it immediately, it was my father's bedroom. My hands suddenly started to tremble, I did not know what to expect and I realised that if I went inside the room there was no going back. Mr Abromeit stared at me for reassurance and allowed me to go inside. My father's bedroom had not been rearranged or organised in an orderly manner, nothing had changed, the last time I had visited his room was yesterday. A finger tapped my shoulder and across the side of the bed there was a hand with blood all over it laying there on the carpet, I checked the other side and to my horror there he was. My father. The father that would always encourage and motivate me, the man that was mentally capable of handling anything he put his mind to, yet all I saw was a man with his body sprawled out on his own carpet. The blood was now dried, but his carpet was a boutique full of it, there was a deep cut within his neck which was now infected and infested with bacteria. My stomach twisted into a knot and I could feel nausea rising from my system, I backed away and vomited heavily on the floor, I could not handle what I saw. I did not even feel like crying, no tears fell, all I was thinking was how cowardly my father had been to commit such an act. But then in my mind, I knew that this was far from the truth.

The way he had killed himself was identified by the kitchen knife, his body was found in the kitchen but the soldiers took his body upstairs to his room because the kitchen floor was wet and they did not want to stain the body. I did not believe what came out of Mr Abromeit's mouth when he explained this, but when the evidence was displayed in front of me, I took it all in and went along with it. To me, something was not adding up, they mentioned my father committed suicide in the kitchen but they had soldiers come to check up on him every day. So, if they were checking up on him why had it taken Mr Abromeit over thirty minutes to discover he was dead? It did not make sense; they would have heard a scream or a shout from somewhere especially if they were close to the house. And also, what troubled me was how they managed to get into the house if that was the case, that was an intrusion, but my main issue was who ordered these soldiers to keep tabs on my father every single day when he refused to close his business down, was it, Goebbels? The Fuhrer? I could not think of anyone else who had the power to do that, unless......no it could not be her, she would never do that, but what if it was her? Is that why she had reacted that way yesterday? If my mother was involved in this, I swore to God right there and then, that she would have to not only explain to me what the hell was going on but she would dearly pay for whatever act she committed. But that was just a theory, I doubted the fact it could be her, maybe there was a misunderstanding. I just did not know, all the explanations I was receiving left right and centre were not making any sense to me.

Each soldier present at the scene was taken outside to continue handling the crowd growing larger outside, I stared out the window and noticed reporters parked outside probably trying to get a report on the situation at hand. My mind was still boggled about my father's sudden death, I wanted to look again at his body but I was advised to keep away, I did not want to argue since the more attention we drew the worse the murder scene would be to the public eye. News spread about my father's suicide a day after I arrived at his house, I was allowed to stay at his home for a while after I explained to Mr Abromeit my struggle with my mother, he agreed to my statement and advised me to not visit my father's bedroom or the kitchen because they were part of the murder scenes. I promised to not be reckless and decided to sleep in one of the available guest rooms down the hallway, there were still soldiers outside the gate for my protection but deep down it was for making sure the corpse would be escorted out of the house without any interference. Once the day had passed, I decided to head to the shop to get some snacks because there was no food in the house, I was given the privilege by my mother to come back home but I decided against it because I had to keep away from her for a while.

A soldier that was located outside my father's house demanded where I was heading, I replied saying I was just heading to the shops to retrieve some items, he signalled one of his comrades to follow me. The man never told me his name while we went to the shop but his appearance was bulky and muscular, he had dark brown hair and hazel eyes, his chin was like the bottom of a truck and his face was not chubby but not slim either. To add to the fact, he never uttered a word to me on our way there, it wasn't until he ordered for me to stroll ahead of him while he surveyed the area. I recognised one of the stores and entered inside to pay for some food. Something caught my attention as I entered inside, on one of the newspaper racks was a bold front-page headline saying:

"FAMOUS JEWISH BUSINESS MAN COMMITS SUICIDE IN HIS LUXURIOUS HOME IN MUNICH!!"

I sighed but went to read the first few pages before putting it back, that was until I spotted that my mother had made a statement about it. Why would she do something so stupid? Scanning her section, she said, "My ex-husband and I had a divorce back in 1932, we had our differences and he was so committed to his religious customs. And I respected that however, I believe that Jason was a poor soul who did not know what he wanted. We had not talked for a while but the last time we talked was just a few months ago, he wanted to check how our daughter was doing, however, he told me that something was troubling him and that he could not handle the mistreatment from the SS. I did not understand what he meant by that, but I felt like whatever that was troubling him that day caused Jason to hit his breaking point. I would never in a million years ever imagine Jason to do that, from how close I was with him, that was never a thought. I mourn for him every day and I know right now he is resting somewhere safe." I laughed out loud then covered my mouth, turning around I saw some customers including the owner pause to glare at me, I apologised and put the newspaper back. What was her motive for putting out something like that? It was not benefiting her nor our family, I mean if that was what she was thinking about, but to be honest, it was hard to know how mother processed things, she was a mysterious woman. There was no denying the fact that she was hurting, that used to be her husband at one point, but I feel like she put that out there to bring more attention to herself; well, she could do whatever suited her. I was not going to be involved, and neither was Mia, she did not deserve this right now. Mia was close to our father as well as me, it would make accurate sense for mother and Mia to be mourning. But deep down I believed that there was more to this suicide than everyone claimed it to be and I was going to find out.

CHAPTER 8

THE DAY I FEARED HAD come, 15th September 1935, the day the policy was about to be issued through the German Reich, I remember it very clearly. It all started on the radio, I was staying at my father's house, however, I decided the day before on the 14th of September to visit my family only because my sister was worried about my safety according to a phone call from my mother. I wondered if the lies were worth it but I needed to know how Mia was doing, so on that same Saturday, I left with my bicycle indicating to the remaining soldiers who were still there at the main gate that I would return. Throughout my journey back, I kept thinking that if my father had lived to see the policy come to pass would it be worth it? Was that the reason? I hope not because that would be the most foolish excuse he would be giving if I met him in the afterlife. I smiled slightly to myself, even thinking about him gave me goosebumps, that was not going to exclude the fact that I was not going to get to the bottom of this, he was MY father, and I was HIS son. This was no revenge, I did not believe in that, what I had faith in was justice and justice had to be achieved no matter the cost.

A LOST SOUL: THE REVELATION

Once I arrived in Berlin, I noticed more soldiers showing up near the railroads for a particular reason, what was going on? Along the railway station, the soldiers who were a part of the SS troops were packed together as if they were all waiting for the train to come. I ignored it and kept cycling, it did not involve me so it did not matter, I cycled down the shortest route to the high street and took a left turn to my neighbourhood and parked my bicycle next to the house steps. There was a crowd of people along the pavements dressed all fancy nice suits and dresses heading to probably party, you would not dress up for an occasion and not go to the best of cabarets. I had never been or have tried to go, my conscience has always told me that it was not suitable for young men my age, but appropriate for grown-ups. I shook my head smiling and climbed up the stone steps; once I reached the front door, I hesitated and then scanned the windows, no one was there, so I thought. Maybe I was dreaming, I coughed harshly swallowing the phlegm in my throat and proceeded to knock lightly waiting for someone nice to open the door.

My visit back to my mother's house was not as pleasant as I thought, but who was I to know that what I had said hurt her? The person who opened the door for me was none other than Beatrice. When she saw me, she instantly braced out her arms to hug me, and I did not stop her. The aroma coming from her smelt like peaches and honey, I would have held onto her longer if not my sister who was standing behind her coughed-on purpose splitting us from both ends. Mia did not even bother to glance at me when I strolled in nervously, I tried to reach her hand but she slapped me away, there was so much pain in her eyes that it dawned on me what explanation mother had told her when I had left. Nothing in the house had changed, everything from the vase to the sofa in the living room was meticulously cleaned to perfection, I was expecting to come home to a torn apart place full of shattered glass and broken objects. It seemed that my mother's temper was improving in comparison with the unforgettable time when she raged and destroyed most things in the house when she divorced my late father.

Sitting down in silence, I asked Beatrice, who was still dusting away at the bookshelves, if they had all heard the news about my father, it was after I spoke those words that Mia rose quickly from the chair and ran upstairs without saying a word. I felt guilty, she had just lost a father, me bringing it up was not helping so I tried to drop the matter however Beatrice decided to face and report her side of the story, "Well, Master Matthew your mother and sister were relayed a message from an unknown soldier from the SS about the tragic news, Mia could not control her emotions let alone hide them at that moment. That poor girl cried as if she had lost life itself however your mother did not cry, weep or even react, I knew that she was trying to remain presentable in front of the SS soldier, so it made perfect sense." I thought about the last few words Beatrice had mentioned; if mother was not acting anyway about it that meant to me that she had heard the message before. My mother always reacted a certain way when it came to deaths, after my grandmother died four months ago, her mother, she cried right there when she heard the news, gripping onto the stair pole not knowing what to do. This meant that if she did not sob or show any emotion when it came to my father's death, she was either involved or she was relayed the information beforehand. The question that kept playing in my mind was if she knew before I arrived at my father's house or after.

Two hours had passed since I arrived, and my mother had not shown her face to me yet, but Beatrice assured me that she was in the house. I had grown tired of lying on the chair listening to the radio, tomorrow was a big day, the day when the Nuremberg Laws would become law in the country, but all that was on my mind was my father. I wanted to pray but I had not prayed in an exceptionally long time, Beatrice who was making lunch was in the kitchen creating a new recipe for her dish collection, the smell whiffed past my nose and I closed my eyes dreaming about what wonderful plate of food she was going to serve us today. Licking my lips, the drool from my mouth made its way to my shirt creating a dark patch stain, I examined and struggled to wipe it off, it was no use, I needed to wash it off with water however I was worried it would make it much worse on my clothes. Shrugging my shoulders, I stretched my body out almost clicking my bones which suddenly began to rattle like a snake being charmed by a mellow tune. I rushed up the stairs heading to the bathroom when I heard a slight noise coming from down the corridor once I reached the top. I pretended to open the toilet door which creaked ever so loudly, the noise subsided and I used that time to follow where the noise was coming from, it started to get louder and louder when I made it to my mother's room. The door was half-open but mostly closed, looking carefully in the gap I could identify my mother faced backwards with a phone handle to her ear, she was speaking to someone but I had no clue who it was. Leaning my head closer, I pressed my ear near to the door and managed to piece some of the phrases she was lamenting on the phone about, that was until I heard my father's name, she referred to him as Jason.

"I do not understand why you had to wait till now, this could have been handled another way......and no this was not the wisest of choices, this has created not only a public scene for Jason but my family as well. I understand what you are saying but you need to just be able to see my view on this matter, I will not allow my name to be tarnished in your wrongdoings, this is not good for you, and not good for me, I do not care how you do it but just please get it sorted because..."

And then I heard a loud shout from downstairs, it threw me off guard, I almost stumbled from the grip on the door handle losing my balance, I placed my right foot first helping me balance my body out against the carpet surface. I was not going to fall, not this time.

"Ms Schmidt, the food I have made has been fully prepared, shall I leave your food on the table?"

"Leave it there Beatrice, I will be heading downstairs very soon, I have a meeting coming up in the German Reich so I will be leaving in an hour."

"Yes, ma'am."

"Beatrice, is my son still downstairs because I need to greet him before I leave?"

"Erm...Ms Schmidt he is in the toilet..."

"Thank you, Beatrice, that will be all, just make sure my food is left on the table."

That was when I knew my time was up, I tiptoed as fast as my long legs could take me back downstairs without making a sound, however halfway down the stairs I remembered I originally had come to go to the toilet. I quickly rushed back upstairs and went slowly inside closing the toilet door. Using my hand to flush the imaginary urine, I intentionally closed the door flamboyantly to make sure my visit to the toilet was true. I needed to make sure I was not viewed as suspicious especially if my mother was losing trust in me, she did not have to say it directly in my face, she showed it indefinitely through her actions. I did not know who to believe anymore, I could not trust no one but myself. It was the only sane thing to do, even during the lunch period my mother sat there opposite me on the table eating as if nothing had happened to my father. The expression on her face was bland, her composure was evident and her eyes were empty, I had to control myself from doing something to her I was going to regret, that was when my sister who was sitting at the head of the table pushed her plate away and grabbed my arm. Confused by her actions, I allowed her to take me like a stray puppy found by her new owner; she took me to the back garden and closed the gateway, using the key from the counter to lock it fiercely. Letting go of me, she suddenly distanced herself while I continued to stare at her in bewilderment, questions were building in my mind, and I did not understand why she was doing this at this moment of all times. Before I could even speak, she pressed herself against me and wrapped her arms around my body, for some reason I did not hug her back, I could not, even though she was my sister I had no emotions to share.

"Matthew...I.... I am glad you came back...we all missed you, even if our mother does not show it...I missed you...very much."

"Missed me? I think you have got your words mixed up Mia, none of you missed me, you are angry at me, both you and mother."

"No! I do not know about mother, but I am not, I.... I can never be angry at you because......because...."

"Because what? Mia, please tell me what is on your mind."

"Because.... because Matthew...I...."

"Mia, I have something I need to tell you..."

"Matthew......because......I......love..."

"MIA LISTEN TO ME."

"I......I am listening Matthew; you do not need to raise your voice at me."

"I need to tell you something about mother, and this is for your good."

"Did she do something to you? Is it something she said that night?"

"Yes and no, when I tell you this, I know it will be hard to believe at first but I will break it down for you to understand whether you believe me or not. Remember that day when I asked you for mother's keys? It was the same day when you told me that Beatrice was in that car accident."

"Yes, I remember perfectly, is it something that involved with what you needed in mother's room?"

"Well, I lied to you saying mother told me to retrieve it, however, to be blunt with you, what I wanted to take from her room is what I am about to explain to you. As you know mother is involved with the Fuhrer. Before I knew about this document, Mr Goebbels had visited our house to hand it over to her."

"But she was not at home I assume?"

"Correct, which brings me to my next point, I wanted to know why he could not give it to me, but his excuse was that it was confidential information. Likewise, the document was a haven for the party so giving it to me would be diabolical, now mother eventually received the package the day after by a soldier who arrived at our house once again, no surprise there."

"So how does this correlate with you wanting the keys?"

"Like I said before it is a concealed document, no one in this house but mother was supposed to read it, so where does mother hide her work? In her room. And as we both know only Beatrice has been given access to clean mother's room until you surprised me by saying you knew where it was which helped massively. Once I opened the document, I found something genuinely concerning that applies to what is about to happen tomorrow in Germany."

"What is it? Should we be concerned?"

"We need to be more than concerned Mia, it was a policy the Fuhrer had decided to implement involving a law called the Nuremberg Laws, which put it simply any Jew who were related to their Jewish grandparents would be arrested and imprisoned. The ideal is you need four German grandparents or ancestors to be classified as a German Citizen."

"But father does not have four German grandparents.... wait.... are you assuming...?"

"You figured it out? Yes, it is true. Father's death is related to this, I was with him a day before he passed, I told him about it that day, moreover, father reported to me that he was being harassed by SS troopers many weeks beforehand which began to get aggressive. In my opinion, I feel this is no coincidence, father did not commit suicide, they all staged it to look like that, and mother was the only one who knew where father was staying besides us. Fast forward, now father is dead. It was odd to me before but my fears seem to be coming into fruition. Especially when I arrived home today because I caught mother on the phone with someone..."

"With whom? Did you recognise the voice?"

"No, but it was a man on the other end, and they were discussing keeping something a secret and that she does not want any attention drawn to her..."

"Are you trying to insinuate that mother was involved in father's death? But why?"

"Maybe, but I am not sure. All I need you to do right now is store what I have told you but do not tell Beatrice or anyone, including your friends. The fewer people who know about this, the better for me, and you."

"Understood, I believe you, but do you think our mother is capable of mixing up in a serious situation like that?"

"Mia if there is one thing for certain, never underestimate mother, there is more to her than meets the eye, remember that well."

As we emerged from the garden and approached the house, Beatrice who was outside cleaning the stone steps queried with us where we had gone off to, Mia beamed at her saying we were just discussing the upcoming Olympics next year in the garden, I forced a smile showcasing my white pearly teeth. Beatrice came up to me and closely examined my face, I was thrown off guard, she then raised her hand and I instantly flinched expecting the worse but then as soon as I opened my eyes, I realised she was rubbing my blonde curly hair roughly. Giggling to herself, Beatrice resumed back to her task and informed us to head back into the house, I sighed and rubbed the sweat off my face and turned to Mia who had a similar expression.

CHAPTER 9

DURING THE END OF 1935, the policy that Hitler declared on the radio had escalated, the Nuremberg Laws reduced Jews to second class citizens because of their so-called "impure blood". Jewish communities were viewed as having impure bloodlines and the new laws taught schools, organisations, ceremonies and even religious systems about anti-Semitism in German Culture making sure it was engraved in millions of minds. Most Germans kept quiet about the animosity occurring in Munich, Berlin and Hamburg, often benefiting when Jews continued to lose their jobs, careers and businesses. Persecution escalated dramatically as the police were given authority to arrest homosexuals and compulsory abortions were administered to women considered to be "hereditarily ill". Not only was this viewed as sickening to the remaining sane people left standing in German society but there was a realisation that there was nothing that could be done as this was how the world operated to them now.

Now the year was 1936, the Third Reich on show, Hitler's anti-Semitic rhetoric has been met and has turned many Germans against the Jews. This has caused a divide amongst the Germans and the Jews.

A LOST SOUL: THE REVELATION

The month was August and it was almost the closing day of the 1936 Summer Olympics, officially known as the Games of the XI Olympiad, where an international multi-sport event held from the 1st to 16th August 1936 in Berlin, Germany. Berlin had won the bid to host the Games over Barcelona at the 29th IOC Session on 26 April 1931. There were approximately 3,632 athletes that participated in the game, around 3,632 men and 331 women, the events were 129 in 19 sports and 25 disciplines. The Summer Olympics in Berlin gave the Nazis a platform to project a crafted image to the world, however despite all the boycotts, the games were a success. However German spectators cheered for a black athlete, a man named Jesse Owens from the USA, he went to win four gold medals surprising not only the Fuhrer but infuriating him as well. Meanwhile, Matthew, Mia and Emilia Schmidt were sitting in the top area opposite where the Fuhrer was seated, there was a look of distaste in Hitler's eyes and Matthew noticed it during the fifteen days.

It was the last day of the world-known Summer Olympics, 16th August 1936, we were making our way back to the Olympiastadion Berlin for the final acts. I came to the stadium first thinking that the Olympics would be disappointing and not the spectacle everyone believed it would be, but after witnessing that man Jesse Owens sweep those gold medals, I realised the talent other countries were displaying to the world. The fury the Fuhrer showed amongst the people during the award ceremony made me smile. Whoever the man was his skin was black, and he was of African heritage, this not only made me question the so-called "Aryan Race" Hitler so proudly spoke of, but it showed Jesse Owens was not just relying on his physical abilities but his mental and emotional tenacity which kept him going till he reached the finish line. When he won his fourth medal, I was one of the people in the crowd that stood out of my seat cheering him on and applauding him for his efforts. It was remarkable and beyond belief that a man, no, a black man from another country embarrassed our athletes in Germany. It was entertainment at its finest. My mother who was glaring at the time, hissed at me to sit down but I ignored her while Mia tried to contain her laughter. My mother rose from her seat and stormed off sulking. I watched her leave, not caring about how she felt since my trust in her had diminished.

Sitting in our usual seats, I examined the stadium and my eyes widened when I saw a parade of Nazis marching from the sidelines holding up the famous Swastika sign painted on the bloody red flag. So, this was the show they were going to end on, it annoyed me because they were putting out their agenda against the Jews just like they did among the games with the fellow Jewish athletes from other countries while some did not show up knowing about Hitler's reputation. Every time I saw a soldier all I could think of was my father, who was ruled out for suicide when in actuality behind closed doors he was brutally murdered by the SS troopers, but of course, I was still investigating the matter. But, on the other hand, what was the point? Even if I did find proof, it was not as if the suicide verdict would be re-examined. All I could do now was try to protect the only thing that mattered to me, and that was my sister Mia.

The trumpets were blown, drums were played and the soldiers stopped marching while the crowd fell silent, upon the podium stood the Fuhrer still with that proud look on his face; I could not stand it. Each soldier saluted shouting the usual phrase as did the crowd, Hitler then coughed and saluted before saying a few words and with that he walked off. The final day began and I sat back contemplating how this all would end, how long was this government going to last? How long was my mother going to keep hiding secrets from her children? For some odd reason, the gut feeling I had was rising in me again, the feeling that none of this was going to get better and that there was nothing I could do to stop it.

I had moved back to live in my old house last year, my mother's family mansion, because the building my father had lived in had gone over its tax due date and no one was willing to help solve that issue which angered me. I did not even have a job. Not yet.

Three days after the Olympic games, I was cycling back from my work appointment with my mother giving her the paperwork to be a part of the government. After what had happened to my father, I decided that maybe it was best for me to start working instead of continuing being in education. It was a difficult decision to make but I knew that it was for the best. My mother informed me that her associates would review the papers and give me an answer within the following weeks. The main reason I was attempting to do this was because I was going to turn nineteen very soon, and I already finished school four months back, my results had come and I was bewildered that I did exceptionally well. My mother, who also received the report from my former headmaster congratulated me by taking Mia and I to a fancy restaurant not far from where we lived which had just opened before the Olympics had begun. I was happy for the time being, but I still had no faith in her, I already knew she had ulterior motives, so I was playing along with her game, but in truth, I still wanted to pursue my career within the government and I was much tougher than I was a year ago, much tougher. My sister had just celebrated her seventeenth birthday on the 10th of August. What surprised me was that she did not sit with us during the day but went to join her friends towards the back of the arena. The girl was growing under my nose and I was trying not to notice, it was much weirder hanging around her like we used to when we were little children because of what she confessed to me back in my room a day before her birthday:

"Matthew, are you busy? If you, are I can speak to you about this later."

"Well, I am finishing the paperwork I need to give to mother very soon but I can talk to you."

"Erm, I can just talk to you later, it is better to focus on that than me."

"Well, now I have lost focus, what is it that you want to tell me, Mia?"

"Erm...this may sound weird but I was thinking that you and I can just maybe sit with each other in the stadium without mother being around. But if you do not want to, we can go to the movies, or go to eat somewhere nice."

"Wait......where is this all coming from Mia, I thought you were going to spend some time with Roseline, Gertrude and Halina? Why this sudden change of heart?"

"I just want to spend time with you that is all, is that a problem? Can I not spend some quality time with my brother? Is that a crime?"

A LOST SOUL: THE REVELATION

"I understand, but why me? You have never asked me to do this before..."

"IT IS BECAUSE I LOVE YOU! BUT YOU ARE JUST TOO STUPID TO FIGURE THAT OUT!"

I did not know how to respond to that, it threw me off guard, it was not even what she said, it was the fact that she was crying like it was some weight on her chest that she had finally managed to push off her shoulders. Mia wiped her eyes and stood there waiting for me to reply, but I had nothing to say, I turned back to my work and continued to write, I did not bother to face her after that, then all I heard was the slam of my door. Gazing back at the door, I realised that she meant every word.

How long had she been feeling like this?

I did not want to know, but deep down I knew that what she had confessed was immorally wrong and she knew that too. Since that day, my mind had not been adjusting to the change, I wanted to tell Beatrice about it but something in me told me not to, if I did tell Beatrice, she would then tell my mother and once my mother found out that would mean serious assumptions and trouble for the both of us. I rode past my old school and stopped right at the track field, the silver gates were barred shut and there was no one present, I wonder what happened to Mr Fischer, I had not heard from him in the last three months.

Did he quit his job?

I doubted it, that man loved sports, especially track, it was his passion, I mean that was what he revealed to me when I attended the school. There was a loud deep voice echoing down the street. I turned to see a man passing by waving a newspaper in front of a woman's face, she appeared uncomfortable and eventually grabbed it from him paying him some money from her brown purse. Behind him was a stack of newspapers all placed in a large black bag. Was he a newspaper seller? Riding my bicycle towards him, I waved my hand in his direction and I managed to catch his attention, he rushed towards me slamming the newspaper on my chest.

"Sir, are you a newspaper seller or did you just buy those?"

"No young man, I am just doing my job and earning my money through these rough times."

"What is this newspaper you are so eager to sell?"

"Have you not heard? The head of the Olympic Village, Wolfgang Furstner, has killed himself."

"What.... what are you talking about?!"

"Like I said boy, the head of the Olympic Village committed suicide."

"Is there a particular reason why?"

"You have to read the newspaper to find out, that will be 1 ℛℳ please."

I shoved the money into his cracked, pale fingers and snatched the newspaper from his hand, and resumed riding back to my neighbourhood. Along the way there was a large crowd of people holding signs saying Wolfgang Furstner in black, this had to be serious indeed. I did not expect the head of the Olympic Village to get this much support, he must have had a massive deal in the public's eye. I went to the corner of an unknown house and parked my bicycle there in case anyone tried to snatch it from me. Scanning through the first few pages, I read a report stating that he committed suicide but the journalist did not report the cause of the suicide, this brought back memories. My father. It was inconceivable that he would commit suicide and there was no suitable justifiable explanation for a suicide as there usually is, and the instinct in my head already was screaming at me. There were two possibilities I could think of: Wolfgang had some information against Hitler and wanted to spread it but got killed, a murder disguised as a suicide, or he did commit suicide but only because of the strain of living under the severe Nuremberg Laws which marked him as being of Jewish Ancestry. There were no other explanations for his death that I could immediately consider. It made me hate the Nazis even more.

CHAPTER 10

THE MONTH WAS OCTOBER. A few months had passed since the loss of the Olympic Village head, Wolfgang Furstner, it had been indeed tragic. Emilia Schmidt, my mother, the woman who wore more than two masks anywhere we went, the woman I detested yet loved, the person who always turned a blind eye when it suited her, had finally managed to get me a position under her whilst she was participating in the German Reich. The news did shock me but it was almost the end of the year, and I received a message from my mother from Beatrice about the news when I had come home from my evening jog. My reaction was a mixture of joy and fear because now I had a chance to see what my mother did, however, I knew there were certain places I could not visit even if I was her son, but my chance to climb the steps of becoming a politician was now finalised. The only thing I had to do was keep on my toes and not mess up especially under a government-run by a dictatorship, the power Hitler possessed was phenomenal and I was about to witness that first hand once I started. Later that day, my mother and I had a meeting about what I had to wear on a usual basis, and since I worked under her, things would not be out of order because she was working with a family member who she trusted.

What did that say about grandfather? Is that why he decided to cut ties working with his daughter?

There was a party coming up and as usual, my mother was invited but she wanted me to come along because she wanted me to talk to the other politicians there, I was not interested but I knew I had no choice otherwise. The event would take place in a massive house owned by a man named Martin Bormann and his wife Gerda Buch; I had heard of Martin Bormann before, never knew what he did but I knew he was in the Nazi Party. The date schedule was ten days from now, and I was going to start next month, so I heard, but I was relieved that I had time to think before my severe work ethic would take place in November.

The party was nothing new to me. If I had to be honest with you, I came from a wealthy family, all the extravagances and delicacies, I had witnessed them all before. My mother knew everyone in Berlin, and they knew her, way before she even met Adolf Hitler, I mean my family's history was well known. There was nothing left to be said.

I was dressing up in my room deciding which fit would be suitable for me, I examined the look I had in the mirror that I picked out myself, the one I was currently admiring was the black bow tie, the crusted clean white shirt, and the dark black blazer matching the trousers. The fit itself was slim which matched perfectly with my body, however I wanted to remain minimalistic as possible because the dark blue suit I wore beforehand was too appealing to the eye, the black would not attract too much attention which meant fewer people to talk to. There was a loud knock on the door and I allowed the person to come in, it was my sister, she was wearing a charm necklace made out of diamonds with a love heart symbol embedded in between, her dress was a rouge colour matching the dark red heels, she looked unbelievably beautiful. Losing focus on my tie, I shook my head and asked her if mother was waiting for both of us downstairs which she responded with a yes, I nodded and adjusted my bowtie one last time before heading downstairs to join them.

As we arrived to the place, the house itself was stunning, I was even surprised at myself for being a little impressed. There was a queue of fancy vehicles lined up near the front entrance, I did not know if we came late or this was part of the display. A man dressed in white with the swastika emblem was making his way up the stairs which had under it an elongated red carpet like the movies, my mother was staring at him smiling mischievously, I did not know if she knew him or if something was going on between them. And to be honest with you I did not want to know. Our car parked along by the back entrance and we all got out and headed straight to the door, a waiter was waiting and he escorted us inside leading us to the gigantic living room where there were many people present. Surrounded by politicians, celebrities, and important men and women, I did not know how to react, I was nervous, no, I was particularly frightened, I was never known to be the social type but I knew how to handle it well, but in this particular situation, I had no clue.

I was introduced around during the gathering to various people, some people were ex-politicians who were in full-fledged support of the idealisms Hitler displayed to the world, others were current government officials who were in the Nazi Party, and the rest were just well-known actors, actresses and famous guests. Some I recognised and some I did not even bother to look twice at, the atmosphere was indeed a sublime, not only was everyone enjoying themselves but the meals served were boosting people's self-esteem. Departing from my mother and sister, I sneaked to the alcohol section to try some wine, I had never been a fan of alcohol but I had never tasted wine before and I wanted to have some. I went to the waiter who poured a glass for me and I gulped it all down in a rush. The taste was so bitter I started to cough and pat my chest making sure it went all the way down, the waiter stared at me wondering if I was okay or not.

Raising my hand to usher another one, the man warily poured another glass and handed it to me but then his eyes wandered and stopped, I was puzzled by his abrupt pause and then I turned around to see Joseph Goebbels standing right behind me. The waiter bowed lowly and offered the glass to Goebbels without hesitation, I was so confused by the scene I was caught up in, what the hell was happening? Goebbels thanked the waiter and put his arm around my shoulder leading me away from the drink section, I followed his lead trying not to resist, I wondered where he was taking me. From the position we were heading, he was making his way outside towards the front steps where the red carpet was, one of the drivers recognised him and saluted before opening the back of the car to hand Goebbels something. I did not know what it was but it was a black case with the round golden handle attached on top, I squinted my eyes to see what was inside when it was clicked open but his back was turned. Then he gave it back to the driver signalling him to take it inside. Goebbels turned to face me and beamed:

"Are you enjoying the night young man? I have not seen you since the Olympics."

"It is going well sir; it is going splendid as I hoped for."

"Good to hear, now I heard from your mother that you will start working for her next month, am I correct?"

"Yes sir, and I am looking forward to it, I will not disappoint."

"Of course, you will not, or else we would not have taken you, but I do want to know why were you hanging around the wine section? Aren't you too young to be drinking?"

"No sir, I am already nineteen so I am of age to drink, I think so."

"Well, I will have to take my leave soon, I just came to drop something off to someone and now I get the chance to talk to you again."

"I did not see the Fuhrer; did he leave earlier too?"

"No, he is back in his office, I am going to meet him there but keep that secret between us, okay? Well, it was nice communicating with you again, enjoy the rest of the party and tell your mother I said bye."

"Yes sir, I will."

"And one more thing Matthew."

"Yes sir?"

"I am truly sorry about what happened to your father. Your mother had informed me about it on the phone. I wanted to visit your family but I could not because everyone has busy schedules, but I hope you and your sister are doing fine without him."

A LOST SOUL: THE REVELATION

"Thank you, sir, I...I am doing fine...."

"Sorry if I hit a nerve but I mean it, I met him once, he is an extraordinary man, but like I said stay strong, and keep moving forward. Alright, goodnight and I hope to see you at work soon."

By the time he had finished saying that the driver had already returned without the case, and he signalled at Goebbels who headed straight in the back of the car. The driver shut the door and glared at me; I did not know what I had done but I glared back which surprisingly bewildered him. The man shook his head and sighed before heading into the front seat. I watched the vehicle make its way towards the main gate before it began to speed along the main road. I headed back inside searching for my mother and my sister, a hand gripped on me and I whipped around almost hitting the person in the face, I realised that this time it was Mia. I breathed in then out almost shouting at her, she could see the anger in my eyes and sidestepped backwards away from me. I grabbed her hand and pulled her close to my face, she did not budge, she just gazed into my eyes. And that was when I noticed mother, I pushed roughly through the crowd still gripping tightly to Mia's arm until I fell back and saw my mother with someone. My mother was smiling at the person, I let go of Mia and drew myself in to see what was going on, I pushed myself into a passing guest apologising but I did not care who it was. All I was focusing on was the person holding hands with my mother, I hid behind a couple of guests so I could not be seen and then the closer I got I realised who it was. It was him, the man who I saw at the entrance dressed in all white.

CHAPTER 11

THE SAME MAN I HAD seen at the entrance was right there next to my mother, is that why she was smirking in the car? Who was he? And what type of relationship did he have with my mother? I had not seen his face yet but for some reason, I did not want to, and then it began to add up; the late phone calls in the night, the constant going out after work, was she seeing him? And for how long had she been visiting or associating with him? The questions kept piling up in my head, I did not understand why this was so essential but it was, whoever he was I needed to find out because if I did not then my mother may be putting herself in danger. The man suddenly turned in my direction but I had already gone back into the crowd, he must have suspected someone was watching, I saw his face, he had dark brown hair, dark blue ocean eyes, a sharp jawline and a muscular figure. Overall, he was a very handsome man, I would not be surprised if he was hanging around or sleeping with multiple women; my mother was probably one of those people. I went back to find Mia but I realised that I did not know where she was. Did she disappear and head outside? I wanted to leave very badly, I was not enjoying myself at all, I wished my father was here right next to me telling me everything was going to be fine, but in reality, that was never going to happen, never. Gripping onto my head, I heard ringing but I did not know where it was coming from, it was making me dizzy, I tried grabbing for something, an object, a table, a chair but there was nothing there, it was too far away. I did not know what was happening to me, the ringing was getting worse, I tried screaming out for assistance but everyone was still partying and having a great time, their faces were getting distorted and blurry, I could not take it anymore. I just could not. That was when I realised, I was sinking, sinking deep into an ocean I could not swim out of; was I breathing or was I already dead?

"Matthew...Matthew...."

"Matthew, can you hear me everything is going to be okay..."

"I do not think he is breathing......where is the doctor?!"

"Matthew......"

Voices. That was all I kept hearing over and over again, it was frustrating and annoying, why could they not just leave me alone? Where was I? Was I in Heaven or Hell? I did not know. I slowly opened my eyes, and I squinted at the creamy ceiling above me, I tried turning my head to the side and I saw another red pillow next to me. Was I in someone's bed? My body felt stiff, my arms were laying there not moving an inch and my legs felt numb. Struggling to move my legs, I wiggled my toes and it seemed like they were still functioning, that was a relief, now all I needed to do was adjust my arms. I wiggled my fingers and I received the same result. That was perfect, using my right arm against my left leg I tossed and turned to grab onto the pillow forcing myself to push itself upwards. Gripping tightly to the duvet I removed the cover allowing me to slip carefully out of the bed, I was sweating heavily, the drips causing wet patches on the sheets, it was pretty vile. I then grabbed the duvet and used my arms to stand so I would not fall out of the bed, once I managed to adjust to the headboard, I climbed my way out of bed landing on my feet but then my whole body lost composure and I dropped heavily to the floor with a bang.

Ouch.

I waited for someone to burst the door open and waltz inside but nothing happened, I was relieved once again, I crawled to the door before reaching for the handle, it was not too far from me but I had to try harder. Slithering back to the bed I gripped onto the nearest chair and used it as support for me to stand upright, my legs were wobbling and my arms were shaking but I had to persevere and not give up. Adjusting my pathway to the door I gripped tightly to the door handle and turned, the door handle did not budge, what was going on? I tried again, then again and then again, it was not moving, crazy thoughts began whirling into my head, was I being held captive? No, that was impossible, I tried one last time and nothing happened, that was when I knew that the door had been locked but why? Did they think I was going to escape? I scanned the room, there was nothing in here but a desk, a brown chair, a small wooden cupboard and a bed, whoever created this room presented it so eerily, I did not want to be here, it gave me the creeps.

No one showed up to the room which made me question if I had been held captive or not. I do not know how long it had been, two days, three days, a week, I was getting tired of it, really tired of it. Luckily, I found a box of snacks and food in a brown box under the bed however there was no water for me whenever I was thirsty, I was in the bed trying to figure a way out of this scenario but nothing came to mind. My head was still hurting from the party, and I knew that I must have fallen into unconsciousness for a while before waking up to being in this isolated room. Checking through the window, I saw people outside walking and children cycling or running playing along the pavement, that was the only thing that was keeping me sane, but for how long? It was two days later that my question got revealed, I was lying there sleeping until I heard the sudden turn of the handle twist left, my body was already back to normal but my brain was sending warning signals that I had to be careful. A young woman and a middle-aged man strolled into the room; I had never seen them before but they appeared to be ordinary people. That was up until I caught the man holding a weapon, I did not know the name but it was definitely a gun. The man was wearing a casual outfit: a blue shirt with grey trousers while his hair was slicked back with a few strands running down his face; he looked familiar but I could not put my finger on it. On the other hand, the woman was much younger, she must have been either my age or a few years older, she was wearing a dark jacket with a baggy sweater underneath and a slim skirt; she sat on the chair near the desk facing me. Her eyes were a mixture of green and blue, her hair was brown with highlights of blonde and I noticed she had not smiled at all since she had entered the room. The man next to her came closer to the bed and proceeded to talk:

"Do you remember me, boy?"

"I cannot remember but I have seen your face before..."

"I was at the party, the one hosted by Martin Bormann, I was wearing the white suit."

"Wait, you were the man who was with my mother, how do you know her?"

"We have been spending some time together for a while now, why?"

"What do you want from me? And why am I here?!"

"Well to put it simply, I am putting you out of harm's way, well, to be honest, I feel you are getting in the way of my plan. You think I did not see you spying on me at the party?"

"Listen, I was not spying, I was curious to know who you were..."

"And that was your problem, sniffing your nose in other people's business."

"Did you kill my father? Was my mother involved?"

The man's eyes widened and he started to giggle, and then he burst out laughing grabbing onto his stomach thinking that what I said was hilarious. The woman however was not smiling, she was still watching me closely like a hawk ready to strike.

"Of course not, why would I ever kill Jason? That is my brother, one of my closest friends."

"What do you mean closest friends?"

"So, he did not tell you about me? Understandable. I would not have done the same if I was in his shoes. Jason and I grew up together until he moved to Berlin as a teenager and I never saw him again."

"So, what does that have to do with you seeing my mother?"

"Well, my strategy is simple, I want to find out who killed him because I do not believe for a second that it was a suicide.

A LOST SOUL: THE REVELATION

I KNOW he was killed. And your mother knows something, well, she has given me hints, but I have heard many things about you, many things. And I feel you will only get in my way."

"I understand what you mean, but I am trying to find my father's killer too, I can assist you, I promise I can be very useful."

"Sorry boy, but I do not think you will help me at all. Whatever you have is meaningless to me. Your mother has told me everything."

"Did she tell you about Mr Goebbels giving her a document over a year ago concerning the introduction plan to the Nuremberg Laws?"

"No.... she has not.... wait a minute...she knew about that policy before it was implemented by Adolf Hitler?"

"Yes, but I can only explain it to you if you allow me to help you, keeping me up in this house and lying to my mother will not last long. My mother has powerful connections and they will find me soon enough, and if I inform them that a man I saw in the party and his female associate captured me, you will probably never see the light of day again. However, if I help you, I can give you what I had found and how it correlates with my father's passing, and I am going to start working under my mother soon so if I get her trust back, I can relay any information she may never tell you."

The man folded his arms, and gazed at the woman next to him, she nodded in agreement and he nodded back to her, he snapped his fingers and she threw the bedsheets away and drew me out of the bed. I was surprised, she then smiled at me, and ruffled my hair.

"It seems like my cousin likes your charisma. I will agree to your proposal, you remind me a lot of Jason, you have his thought process. If you agree to this, there is no going back, understood?"

"Understood."

"Alright, Lulu, show him to the shower, and make sure he has some fresh towels before he heads in, we have work to do."

The agreement had been made, Lulu pushed me towards the door and patted the man on the shoulder for reassurance, something was bothering him. Once I stepped out of the room, there was a long hallway leading to a room up ahead, the walls were filled with paintings, and bouquets, was this his house? Lulu showed me to the bathroom and I took in the sweet scent, it was heavenly, the bath appeared to be spotless and taken care of well, she pointed to the fresh white towels and left me alone. I went to examine myself in the mirror, I looked terrible, from my hair down to my feet, I laughed to myself, so there were other people out there who cared about my father as well. A memory of my father came instantly in my mind.

Was this what my father had meant when he used to say God brings people into your life for a reason?

CHAPTER 12

THE MYSTERIOUS MAN'S name was called Marcus Rhinestone, and his cousin was called Louise Rhinestone, his father was Louise's father's older brother which is why they are related. Mr Rhinestone gave me a brief history of his upbringings and how he knew my father. I even asked him if I could address him as Marcus instead of addressing him as Mister, which he gladly supported since he hated feeling like he was much older than he was. Marcus was born in Munich, he was raised by his single mother and older sister, he dropped out of school when he was seventeen to pursue his career as an actor. Before he made it to the big screens, he met my father in the same neighbourhood, my father lived a street away and they went to the same school. Marcus usually visited my father's house many times when he never went to classes, and my grandfather and grandmother would usually cover for him when his mother was annoyed by his erratic behaviour. My father went to see him at his house sometimes when it came to helping him with school work. Marcus's sister, whose name was Martha had once told him that no matter the circumstances they lived in, they could all achieve their goals if they put their mind to it. This made Marcus become more serious with his talent and branch out to set his plans into action. At the age of thirteen, he found his agent through his sister who had connections to the entertainment industry due to the fact her boyfriend at the time was friends with fellow agents.

Showcasing his talent and hard work, he rose, but so did my father, they were both doing what they loved, however by the time my father turned nineteen, he left for Berlin because he wanted to branch out his business elsewhere. Marcus and my father stayed in contact by visiting each other but after my mother and my father married, Marcus never heard a word from my father ever again. While my father was booming in his business in Berlin, Marcus was travelling the world appearing in movies and theatre with the help of his new agent which was now his cousin, Louise Rhinestone, however, Louise had done other dangerous jobs before she was given the position to become his agent and manager, which intrigued him. That was until he met my mother, not knowing at the time that she and my father had divorced until later on. It was not until my father passed away that he began to fully invest himself with my mother because he wanted to know why he was killed and who the killer was. He did not believe that his best friend committed suicide, that was not who he was.

Our plan was straightforward, each of us had an idea of what our role was going to be for the next few months, the only problem was that whenever a situation out of our control would happen, we would have no choice but to retrace our steps. Marcus' role was to get as much information from my mother as possible, even if that meant visiting my house more often, taking my mother to certain luxury venues in cities, having sex with her, whatever he had to do to make her spill anything to do with my father. The positive thing was that he had been talking with my mother for some years now, so the way she viewed him was very intimate which annoyed me to an extent. Suddenly a dark thought came to my mind. What if my mother was actually involved in her husband's murder? I shook my head. What was wrong with me? I needed to get those stupid thoughts out of my head, but I could not help it. She has been acting different and deep down my father's murder had something to do with it. On the other hand, Louise's role was to spy on my mother's daily routine: where she went on a regular basis, who she visited, when she left work and even staying at Marcus's house to hear their conversations. I did not know how she was going to manage that but after what Marcus informed me about what his cousin used to do back in Dortmund, I decided not to question her methods any further. My role was to find any information during my workplace that seemed to be out of the ordinary and keep a tab on the meetings I would participate in which included anything concerning paperwork I had to get done or secrets I would be given insight to depending on how trustworthy I was.

The instructions did not seem complicated but deep down I knew that it was going to be difficult, not only was I nineteen years old but I was not completely accustomed to how these politicians acted behind closed doors, and I was going to find out soon enough when the time was right. Before November came, I would either leave to visit Marcus and Louise for more instructions in the meantime, but that was not always the case, like I stated before, Marcus Rhinestone was a well-known actor and he had to travel, but luckily the home that he had held me captive in was in Berlin as well. The home was bought a few years ago, so travelling there by bicycle was only around twenty to thirty minutes, Louise was his agent so I did not get time to even see her at all because she was with him most of the time but she would call me when she was less busy or free. Whether it was to update me on what she has found on my mother or just to spend time with me at Marcus's house. Marcus would discuss the plan with me whether Louise was present or not. I would meet Marcus outside or wait after having a phone call a couple of minutes prior with either Louise or Marcus on when the driver will arrive.

The first time Louise visited my house was very unexpected, it had been almost five days after I was released from Marcus' house after they abducted me. I explained to my worried and infuriated mother that I had been staying with James for a few nights, but I had to make it add up to the party, so this is what I told her: After I passed out, I was carried by Marcus Rhinestone to a spot outside the party entrance and he waited for me for a few hours before returning with a glass of water. I woke up dazed and asked him who he was which he responded with Marcus Rhinestone, he said he knew my mother and was with her a couple of minutes ago until he noticed me faint in the living room. I told him that I was leaving and he asked where but I did not tell him. I lied to him saying I will return in a few hours but I did not, I made my way to James' place and told him not to report to my mother I was staying at his house which he fully agreed. When she heard my story, I could tell she wanted to believe me but, in her eyes, it stated otherwise, she picked up the phone and called James' mother who said I had been staying at their house for five days which shocked my mother. She then put the phone down and scowled at me saying I should next time inform her if I was going to stay at any of my friends' homes. I mean I did a great job concealing the truth because James' mother was also in on it, even if she did not know the real reason why I had disappeared either, it was better that way since Marcus ordered me to do this before I left his house:

"No one, and I mean no one should know that you were here, the only individuals who should have any idea where you were after the party is Lulu and I, got it?"

Those words echoed loud and clear in my brain every day as if he was daring me to mess up, not going to happen, I was careful and unlike the rest, I trusted nobody.

Louise had knocked on my door consistently as if she was trying to break her way in, it was not until Beatrice, who was busily sorting out my mother's bookshelves, stormed downstairs opening the door about to shout at whoever was disturbing from outside. It was Beatrice's scream that caught all our attention excluding my mother, she had gone out to visit a particular "someone" in Berlin, well, I already knew who she was referring to, it had to be Marcus of all people. I was the first person who hurried to the entrance while Mia trudged along behind me. Mia seemed lazy compared to how charismatic she usually was, I could not blame her, it was the winter season, it was snowing, and there was nowhere else to go without feeling cold. Louise burst past Beatrice and eventually saw me, she ran up to me and at the spur of the moment hugged me tightly, Mia's eyes widened and she came to life. Her body sprang into action and she tried to rip Louise off of me like she had just spotted a leech attached to my skin.

Everyone was out of control, Beatrice was still baffled by Louise showing up in the living room, Mia was disgusted that another woman was caressing me, and I was trying to keep my composure picturing myself on a beautiful island far away from here but it was not working. All I could hear was shouting, questions, shouting, questions and more shouting, it was giving me a headache and I was like a volcano erupting, my head was about to explode. I could not take in this environment anymore. Pushing Louise away from me, she instantly grabbed my arm twisting it behind my back, and forced me down onto the carpet floor. All I could view was a frightened Mia backing away from Louise and Beatrice heading to the phone trying to call someone, was it the police? I did not know, but this incident was getting out of hand, and I needed to put a stop to this. And then it happened. Beatrice dropped the phone, Mia stopped moving, and I shut my mouth.

Why did I stop myself from speaking?

To put it simply, I had a pistol pressed to my head, and Louise was holding it, not only did the room go silent, everyone was in deep fear. I was lifted from the carpet with the gun still at my scalp, and then Louise signalled Mia and Beatrice to sit on the sofa, Beatrice raised her hands and gladly obliged and Mia was about to say something but I stared at her dead in the face and she got the message. As they sat down, Louise also ordered me to sit on the sofa opposite Mia and Beatrice. I followed her instructions without hesitation, she went to sit next to me and put her arm around me with the gun now aimed at my temple. I was not wrong after all, Louise was not crazy, she was a complete psychopath.

A LOST SOUL: THE REVELATION

No one had uttered a word for almost ten minutes, Beatrice was still trembling, Mia was trying to contain her composure, Louise was relaxed next to me, and I was wondering when she was going to lay the gun down from my side. Mother would not be home until 11:00 pm which was bad news for all of us, if only I could say something to Louise that would not impact negatively on Mia and Beatrice, I did not want anyone to be hurt, let alone be shot. My eyes wandered all around the room, there had to be something I could use or better yet distract Louise but there was nothing, I turned slowly to Beatrice who was only a few metres away from the phone, she met my gaze and nodded.

"What are you both doing?"

I became alert and whipped my head back to face Louise, she had a curious expression on her face, Beatrice, on the other hand, put her head down in fear worried about what Louise was going to do to her, she was not the only one who was frightened either, I was scared as well. The finger was still gripped on the trigger, if she pulled it then I knew I was going to die in an instant, there was no other way around it, we were either going to sit here in silence and wait for something miraculous to happen or one of us needed to be brave and end the awkwardness in the room. If that had to be me, so be it.

"Louise, I need to ask you why we are all sitting here, and why you are holding me at gunpoint?"

"No particular reason, maybe because it amuses me."

"Well, that is not a very good answer, actually that sounds like a ridiculous statement to make."

All of a sudden, I felt the gun press deep into my side, I winced and stared at Louise, there was a dark expression across her face and she did not seem pleased by my response.

"You are not in the best predicament to be telling me what is good or not, you do realise I can shoot you whenever I please, so be careful when you raise your tone or act smart in front of me Matthew."

Gulping twice, I nodded and put my hands on the chair, she was right about two things, she did have the power right now and she did have my life in her hands, the only problem was how long was she going to keep up this foolish act? There was no way she was going to kill me, Marcus would never allow it, if he heard about this incident right now, he probably would have shown up here and stopped Louise from doing something reckless.

"Then why are you here? Are you testing me?"

"Testing you? Why would you think that?"

"Maybe because if Marcus was here, you would not be holding a gun to my side, it would not be in your best interests to kill me, you need me."

"How would you know how Marcus feels? You do not know him like I know him."

"Well, you are right I do not, but he knew my father and he is my father's best friend so it does matter if you kill his son."

Louise dropped the gun from my side and ordered me to get up, I followed her instructions and stood there not knowing what was about to happen, she then stood up and faced me, I could see the hate in her eyes. What had I done? Then her face relaxed and before I knew what was going on her leg was raised and I felt this terrific pain storm up through my side, I dropped heavily to the floor gripping onto the medial side of my left knee, it was stinging really bad. A rage inside of me exploded and I rose from the carpet floor and swung at Louise's head, she dodged it and gripped tightly to my arm before reversing my whole body anticlockwise, I did not know what was going on and I was not waiting to find out. Using my other arm, I punched her in the stomach and she coughed severely falling back, she then smiled grotesquely at me and rushed towards my direction before tackling me headfirst to the ground. Hitting my head on the table, I felt dazed but the anger in me was rising, she was currently on top of me trying to grab both of my arms, I gripped onto her head and headbutted her in the forehead, I was expecting her to fall back but she did not budge. Shocked at the outcome, I tried again but she did not move, she was just horrendously smiling at me, that was until she started pummelling me in the dust. I was trying my best to shield myself but her fists were coming in way too fast, it was beyond my comprehension. I noticed there was a red mark on her forehead and drips of blood running down from it but she did not care. Struggling to block her attacks, I reversed her legs against her causing her whole body to flip from underneath, I put my arm around her neck and locked my legs around her body. It was working, she could not move, I was grappling her and she was trying to fight back but I knew that she was going to submit any time soon unless she wanted to lose consciousness. I shouted at Beatrice to go call mother, and without hesitation, Beatrice ran to make the call, while Mia gripped tightly to Louise's legs to prevent her from moving against me.

"Louise, listen to me, this is pointless, I do not know why you are here, but you need to leave, you have caused quite a commotion."

"Do....do not tell......me what to do....... I am not going......to listen......to....... you......"

"Fine then, suit yourself, Mia do it now."

Mia folded onto Louise's legs with her arms and pressed roughly against them with her elbows, Louise began to scream in agony, I ordered Mia to keep going until Louise agreed to leave. Louise was not responding as I hoped so Mia pressed even harder, Louise gritted her teeth, I could see the tears rolling down her cheeks, all she needed to do was agree with my terms. The guilt began to settle in but I wiped it away with ease, I was not going to feel sorry for someone who had just held me at gunpoint, I squeezed harder giving her indication that she had no choice. I nodded at Mia and she signalled me the final push, and she pressed her elbows deeper, Louise could not take the pain anymore and yelled her lungs out, she was crying and in tears:

"PLEASE, PLEASE LET GO OF ME!! I WILL LEAVE, I PROMISE I WILL GO!!! I PROMISE, PLEASE JUST STOP THIS AGONY, I CAN NOT TAKE IT ANYMORE!!!"

"I don't believe you. Promise me you will leave."

"I PROMISE SO PLEASE JUST LET ME GO!!!!"

Mia let go of her legs and I released my grip on her, she grabbed onto her throat coughing and spitting out blood mixed with saliva onto the carpet floor. Mia then confronted her and Louise stared at her in the face. To my horror, Mia swiftly punched Louise right in her face causing the injured woman to scream out. I ran to Louise who raised her hand to prevent me from touching her, she was grabbing onto her nose. The blood oozed onto the carpet floor, I went to get a napkin from the kitchen and automatically gave it to her. Louise grabbed it from me and put it over her nose, I glared at Mia, who was confused by my expression, she must have thought she was doing something heroic but it had been the total opposite. I was not impressed. Beatrice returned to the living room and whispered in my ear that my mother was heading back home, I explained to Beatrice to escort Louise out of the house and to make sure not to aggravate her even further. Beatrice stared at Louise and turned back to me and assented, she picked up Louise by the hand and took her carefully to the entrance area. Once I heard the door slam shut, I rested my head on the sofa and my eyes began to flutter, I was tired and needed to rest for a while. Closing my eyes, I recapped everything that occurred and erased them from my thoughts, all I wanted was peace.

Was that too much to ask?

CHAPTER 13

AFTER THE ALTERCATION with Louise, I was treated by a doctor. He was a close associate to my mother, his name was Doctor Bechstein, I had never seen him before but apparently, he used to come to treat my sister and I when we were much younger. The doctor confirmed I had a minor injury at the back of my head from the fall when I hit the table, he said to me I was lucky I did not hit the edges because I would have been dead. The treatment did not take long at all, I was relieved that my mother had come home like she said because I thought it was all going to be a lie. Beatrice has not been the same since that day, it had left a scar on her, every time she hears a ring at the door, she grabs the broom with her to defend herself from whatever creature is outside. On the other hand, Mia was becoming more confident than usual, it seemed like she was not going take any softness from no one anymore, not even me, and of course, she was getting more physical.

And me?

Well, I am still the same as I have always been, I had discussed the incident with Marcus who was indeed heartfelt by the situation but annoyed that Louise would expose herself like that in front of my family. When I queried with him about what stimulated this behaviour, he replied saying that it was complicated but in simple words, he said sometimes Louise was triggered by certain memories from her past causing her to act differently when around people. To me it felt like she had more than one personality, maybe she was possessed by something, I did not know and I was not going to risk getting deep into it. Before I ended the call, Marcus stated to me that if Louise attempts to do anything reckless like that again I should personally call him in case things get out of my hands. Something in me asked if she was living with him which he replied no, he explained that she had her own place in Berlin not too far away from him but she would stay over at his if they had to travel or get work sorted. Once I ended the call, I sat back on the sofa and reminisced about the woman screaming, Louise was crying out for help, I wondered what was really going on.

I arranged a private meeting with Marcus Rhinestone the next day to get his permission to visit Louise as he was very protective of his cousin. Marcus was hesitant at first but after my consistent persuasion, he finally allowed me to go see her that same day calling her beforehand just in case anything went left. Louise lived thirty minutes away from Marcus which was not bad for me because I had taken my bicycle along the way. Marcus handed me a package of biscuits to supply me for my journey just in case I was hungry, he was incredibly open compared to how he usually was which surprised me, but I accepted and headed along to my destination. The journey was peaceful which surprised me even more, usually I would see police outside near this area arresting people for crimes such as stealing from shops and stores but it seemed there was no one here, maybe everyone was afraid or times were evolving for our own good; the children were not outside either, it was odd, I was not only baffled by the change of scenery but I was intrigued and curious about what Louise had to say for her animosity a few days ago. It was strange when Marcus mentioned that sometimes she was not herself, it scared me, but I knew maybe this was who she was.

Once I arrived at the street, I parked my bicycle near her steps and went to knock on her door. As soon as I knocked on the door, it instantly opened and I almost fell inside. I gazed up at the person in front of me, it was Louise, she was wearing wide-leg beach pyjamas, it was amazing, she looked amazing. Rubbing my eyes, I tried to stare at her face but what she was wearing was throwing me off, she glared at me and grabbed my ear before dragging me inside. Once we entered her living room, she let go and went to another door before revealing a tray of snacks, I pulled out the biscuits Marcus had given me and she sighed before laying it down on an old-fashioned petite table; the designs were not from this country, it appeared as if it came from America or maybe England. I reached inside the package and hungrily ate the biscuits to erase the image of Louise from my mind, Louise side-eyed me and went to sit down on the red sofa opposite me, she was not angry yet she was not happy to see me. It was as if my arrival was a pain in the foot for her but she was coping with it. I tried smiling to loosen the atmosphere but she did not smile back, I did not know what to do or say, it reminded me of the awkward silence back in my house when she raided it and had a gun pressed to my side. Was she always like this? Abruptly Louise coughed and began to speak:

"So, Marcus told me you came all the way here to see me, so what is the problem?"

"Well, to put it bluntly Louise I was informed that you have an issue with being your true yourself."

"What do you mean "being myself"? Are you saying I have problems?"

"No, no, I will give you a simple example, when you held me at gunpoint, what was the reason if I may ask?"

"As I stated to you before there was no particular reason why I did that, it was a feeling."

"And that is my problem, everything happens for a reason, you cannot be saying you felt like it if you do not do this to Marcus."

"So, Marcus told you this I presume? Is he the one you had this discussion with?"

"Erm......yes.... but......"

"No buts, so are you only here because he sent you? Be honest with me."

"No, I came here out of my own free will, all I want to know is are you okay? Is this the first time you have done this to someone?"

"To be completely open with you Matthew I have done some things that I utterly regretted in the past but I cannot tell you where this all stems from. And that is because I am trying to find the truth too."

"I understand, well I better be going now. At least I know you are doing good."

"Is that all came for? You literally travelled all this way for nothing. But you cannot go because I have some questions for you too."

"Go ahead Louise, I am ready for them."

"How old are you?"

"I am nineteen years old."

"Why should I trust you because I have had my doubts."

"Like I explained to you and Marcus before it benefits all of us if we work together."

"How do you feel about me?"

"Erm.... what do you mean? That question was out of the ordinary."

"It is a simple question, please stop trying to make it sound harder than it is."

"Well.... you are a weird person, you proved that to me when you bombarded my house, but I forgive you, your demeanour is usually off and by that, I mean you do things that frighten me. Overall, I feel you are a monstrous and scary person but deep inside I know that if you allow yourself to trust me more, I will be able to see the kind and loving woman Marcus tells me when he discusses about you."

There was complete utter silence, her expression had changed drastically. She covered her mouth and closed her eyes; I caught her lips forming into a smile. Once she opened her eyes, she stood and came to sit next to me, I did know what to do, and I did not know if she knew either. Turning to face me, she gazed into my eyes and for some reason, she appeared to be more attractive from an up-close angle, I noticed her cheeks where bright red.

Was she embarrassed?

Louise shook her head and embraced me with a hug, what was different about this one compared to the last was she meant this one, it was warm, fuzzy and delicate. Some of her hair was near my face, I tried not to sneeze by pushing my head to the side, I closed my eyes too and hugged her back, she smelt nice, it was a scent that was a mystery to me but it seemed at the same time so familiar. Pushing her body away from me, she whispered something in my ear that drew me to a halt, I stared at her in amazement and she giggled. I did not know how to respond but this was a side I had never seen of Louise. It was freaking me out but at the same time I did not mind it all, she put her finger on my lips and told me that she will try to trust me even if it will take time, I nodded obediently not knowing how to reply, it was as if I was caught in a trance. Letting go of me, she stood up and grabbed my hand before taking me into her kitchen, it was not as huge as her cousin's but she knew how to keep it clean. If I was a maid, I would have no chance. There was a sudden ring, and Louise left me in the kitchen and went to the telephone set, I scouted the kitchen to see if she had any more biscuits but then I remembered she had put a tray in the living room. As soon as I entered, there was a dark expression once again settling on her facial features, she put down the telephone and told me I was going to stay over today. When I asked why she replied saying that she received a call from Marcus saying that he plans on taking my family to his house today so I should not worry. I agreed with her proposition and went to snatch the biscuits from the tray before heading back into the kitchen with her behind me.

CHAPTER 14

MY NIGHT STAYING AT Louise's house was out of the ordinary, even during dinner I wondered why Marcus would invite my whole family including Beatrice to visit his house, what was he trying to accomplish? So not only did my sister know who he was, so did Beatrice too, and what if they drew connections with Louise to Marcus? What then? I was still thinking about this when I was laying in my bed in the guest room, that was until I heard a slight knock on the door and I wondered why she was outside. Allowing her in the room, Louise came in with a glass of milk and biscuits, she had a concerned look on her face, and I was not dazzled by it, maybe she already figured out what I was so worried about or maybe she just wanted to see me. Louise sat on the edge of the bed and offered me the glass of milk which I gladly accepted; I refused the biscuits because my stomach was already full from the meal she served me prior. Louise rose to her feet and was about to leave but then paused. Turning back to face me, she told me if I wanted to stay in her room for the night but I already knew where this was going, she wanted comfort and was lonely, but I was not going to fall for it, I politely refused and said that I needed to sleep for tomorrow. Then all of sudden, she began pouting and slammed the door fiercely almost damaging the hinges, I pulled the duvet over me and decided to close my eyes, I was sleepy and I could feel the drowsiness settling in, I had to sleep because if I did not, I would not be prepared for tomorrow. An hour had passed, and I slowly opened my eyes. Something was bothering me, but I did not know what it was. I shook my head and placed my head softly on the pillow case.

I just needed to rest more.

As I was huddling next to the pillows, I felt something warm next to me, and it did not feel like the mattress at all, I slowly opened my eyes again and realised that it was still dark. How long had I slept for? Rubbing my eyes, I tried to move but I was stuck, I could not shift myself towards the edge so I could turn on the light, something was holding onto me and I did not know why. I placed my hands down the sheet and felt skin, they were fingers, soft and warm, and they were wrapped around my body, I abruptly freaked out and fell off the bed landing painfully on my backside. Rubbing my head, I went to switch on the light and to my dismay, I found a curled-up Louise on the left-hand side of the bed, I was annoyed but at the same time I was sympathetic and understanding. I did not get what her problem was but I knew deep down she was beginning to feel comfortable around me.

Tapping her softly on the arm, she yawned and squinted her eyes, smiled and tried to hug me, I moved away and headed towards the door, there was no way I was sleeping there, I just could not. As I reached for the door handle and turned it trying to not make any noise, the door eventually creaked and I gritted my teeth struggling to control the urge of opening it wide. The more I pushed the door, the more noise it made,

I managed to finally get it to open to the point that I had a chance to squeeze through without causing any disruption. Tiptoeing out the room, I instantly heard Louise talking quietly, I paused and slowly whipped myself around to see if she was still asleep. Phew. There was nothing to be frightened about, as long as I kept the sounds to a minimum, I was fine.

"Please don't go......please don't leave me...please...."

I froze. What did she just say? I was almost at the centre of the stairs across the hallway until I heard it again, I did not want to leave but deep down I felt as if someone was watching me. As if bloodshot eyes were peering and staring at me from all directions, I shivered and whirled around to see from the distance Louise tossing and turning in the bed muttering phrases to herself. Feeling sympathetic, I exhaled and shook my head, I could not leave her like this, it was scaring me, I made my way back to the room, not bothered now by how much sound my body was making, and shut the door silently. I went to the right side of the bed and threw the covers over me facing the opposite way, I then felt her hands slowly wrapping around my body and I did not feel any repulse or tried to shift her off me, the muttering stopped and I could feel her snuggling her face on my back. I smiled to myself and my eyes wandered to the window, the moon was reflecting off the glass and the light bouncing off into the room, it was like those imaginative and magical dreams you had that you never expected to lay sight on in reality.

The sudden urge to see my family dawned on me, I missed my mother, I missed Mia and for some odd reason I missed Beatrice which was uncanny, this whole world was corrupt but at least I had the people in my life that mattered most. And then he came into my mind, my father, if only he was here too, he was the one I longed for the most, I closed my eyes and tried to erase the thoughts racing through my mind. But I could not, I wanted to see him again, I wanted to know who killed him, I wanted someone to tell me that everything was going to be okay; I just wanted to leave this country and start a better life for myself. And yes, I was not complaining about my position, my mother was wealthy, and I was destined to be wealthy, and so was my sister, but that could not be said the same for all those Jewish businessmen and workers who lost their careers and jobs; they were not okay. The children in the slums who were sitting outside every day waiting for a chance to occur, those people were not fine, the mothers who had to cover their babies in used clothes, the teenagers looting and stealing to make a decent living for themselves, what about their wellbeing? Louise who was still cuddling me whispered to me that everything was going to okay, but was she right? Or was she just saying that just to make me feel better? Deep down I knew that Germany was not going to get any better, I just knew, I was just waiting for my thoughts to come into fruition.

The next morning, I left Louise's house to head back home to Berlin, but before I went, she indicated to me to give this message to Marcus which she folded and put in an envelope, I took it and placed it in my coat pocket. She then told me to stop calling her Louise and call her "Lulu" from now on. It was unexpected but I promised her I would when I felt more comfortable.

The bicycle ride back would take me approximately thirty minutes so halfway I stopped at a shop to buy some snacks in case I got hungry again, it was a wild card to play because

I was not even in the city and I did not want to risk any police questioning where I had been. Luckily when I entered the shop there was no one present, only two young men who were buying newspaper articles from the rack section to the far left. I grabbed as many snacks as I could and paid it right there to the owner, from the expression on his face, he did not appear to be in the best of moods. I quickly gathered the snacks and went on my way leaving the money on the counter. By the time I got outside, I went to the section where I parked my bike but it was gone, I scratched my head wondering who had stolen it and then at the corner of my eye I noticed a young boy riding on a bicycle that resembled mine. He was accompanied by two other girls who also were near two bicycles. I stormed my way towards them and one of the girls alerted the other two children, they ran to their bicycles and hopped on but I had already made it to the boy and grabbed him by the arm squeezing it tightly, he screamed and yelled for his friends to assist him but they had already gone. I let go of him and demanded why he would steal my bicycle. The reply I received sounded so ignorant that I felt sorry for him, I did not even bother to argue, I grabbed my bicycle and placed my snacks in front of the basket attached and headed on my way while the boy was consistently throwing more insults my way. The further I rode away from him, the more silent it became and for some reason, I wheeled back to see if I could see him but there was nobody there.

Once I arrived in Berlin, I decided to make the delivery to Marcus Rhinestone's house like I promised Louise, it would be an extra fifteen minutes but I did not mind because there was nothing for me to do today. The house was as quiet as ever and I caught Marcus about to leave with his driver. As they were heading inside his vehicle, Marcus recognised me from the distance and waved in my direction, the driver saw me as well but he was not pleased. Getting off my bicycle, I strolled as quickly as I could towards Marcus and placed the envelope in his hand, he gazed at me confused, I did not have time to explain so I signalled to him to just read it in the meantime, he nodded and gave it to his waiter who was also present, I didn't even notice him at all. It was like he appeared out of thin air like some sort of deity or spiritual being, he was well composed and fully dressed, he bowed lowly and rushed back inside, closing the entrance door without thinking. Shaking my head, I got onto my bicycle with ease and waited for the car to head towards the gate first while following in suit behind it, I parted ways by the road works and went further down to head back to my neighbourhood.

The one thing that was always presenting itself to me was that I had only two days until I would begin work in the adult world, it sounded scary. I wanted to impress my mother but at the same time, I had a mission to learn things and find out anything that may bring light to the situation that caused my father to be murdered. Whatever it was going to be I needed to be extra cautious of anyone who was associated with my mother politically and financially which included any deposits made to her or involvement with the Nazi Party. Anyone could be a suspect, and Marcus was doing his part, and I had to carry out mine, no matter what happens, this was for the greater good, for my family in particular. The only problem that kept me unsettled regularly was how deep I had to go to understand what was occurring behind closed doors. It kept ringing in my brain every single time I thought about my mother, I was playing a dangerous game, and if I was caught then so be it, but I have to make sure that it will never happen because if it does, I am not putting myself in jeopardy but my whole family too.

The time was now past 5:00 pm, I had arrived back home safe and sound almost twenty minutes ago, I was tired but yet again I was not, I was trying to get prepared once again for what waited for me in the lions' den. Flicking through the Mein Kampf book one last time, I dropped it into the bin and closed the kitchen door. Reading the book over and over made me realise that there was no point dabbling in the book anymore. Every single word was stuck in my head. The knowledge gained from reading Mein Kampf changed every time I read it. It established a power within you that assisted in gaining things the first and the second time you read it. Deep down you would have never expected at all. But now I had memorised every single page as best as I could, the topics Adolf Hitler discussed and shared his views on were embedded deep inside my brain like a permanent scar that will never be removed. It was magnificent in a sense where now that losing was not an option, I used what I had learnt time and time again from Mein Kampf in the workplace, I had to play two different roles, and was it going to be fun? Oh yes, it was, however, I had to make sure I distinguished the factors of his idealistic beliefs from mine, if I got them construed in the same box then I may get lost in what I came to do in that work environment. I checked my watch, it was almost 6:00 pm. What a relief. I had some time to talk to Louise on the phone before Beatrice and Mia got back home, they had both gone to buy some ingredients for the dish Beatrice was going to prepare for us today. I was looking forward to it, my stomach was rumbling and those biscuits had already been devoured before I arrived back. I went on to make the call but there was no answer, I tried again but there was no answer, what was going on? Was she busy or was she doing something important for Marcus? I tried for the final time but there was no answer, I felt frustrated because I wanted to see how she was doing but it did not matter. I placed the phone down and went to switch on the radio, I did not care what was playing or who was speaking, the tiredness was creeping up on me again, it was becoming an issue. Closing my eyes, I thought back to that conversation I had with Adolf Hitler when he first came to my house in 1930:

"How do you feel about the Jews?"

I had no answer for him back then and I probably will never get the chance to speak to him again but knew my answer. I felt the Jews deserved better than what they were facing because I was taught that everyone should be treated the same no matter where they come from. And that was how I truly felt.

CHAPTER 15

TODAY WAS THE DAY, my first day at work, November 3rd, 1936, it was extremely exciting for me because of two main reasons: one because I had finally managed to work in a government environmental setting which was one of my dreams, and the second reason was that my mission was officially beginning. Once my mother and I left the house, we were taken in the car and driven to Munich where my mother's office was, it was surprising because along the way she informed me how the whole Nazi Government worked. According to her, Hitler ruled Germany autocratically by asserting the Führerprinzip which was called the "leader principle", this called for absolute obedience by all subordinates who willingly followed his ideals or those who carried his interests. Mother said Adolf Hitler viewed the government structure as a pyramid, with himself as the infallible leader at the apex. Party rank was not determined by elections, and positions were filled through appointment by those of higher rank. The example she gave was Goebbels, he controlled the media, the arts and mostly propaganda in Germany and his rank was not determined by election but by his loyalty to Hitler. My mother hinted that I should never tell anyone this, but apparently

A LOST SOUL: THE REVELATION

Goebbels has been discussed in private amongst the other members that he may be Adolf Hitler's successor.

The reason it threw me off balance was because I never expected Goebbels to be this close to The Fuhrer unless they were already planning this type of settlement behind closed doors. From the long talk, we had in the car mother revealed to me somethings I had never even heard of. Let us just say that the successive Reichsstatthalter decrees between 1933 and 1935 abolished the existing Länder known by my mother as the constituent states of Germany and replaced them with new administrative divisions, the Gaue, governed by Nazi leaders. The change was never fully implemented, as the Länder were still used as administrative divisions for some government departments such as education. This led to a bureaucratic tangle of overlapping jurisdictions and responsibilities typical of the administrative style of the Nazi regime. What surprised me more was the intel of how most Jewish civil servants lost their jobs in 1933, except for those who had seen military service in World War I. Members of the Party or party supporters were appointed in their place. As part of the process of Gleichschaltung, the Reich Local Government Law of 1935 abolished local elections, and mayors were appointed by the Ministry of the Interior. This was a lot to take in and before I could respond we had already arrived at her office. Not only had I learnt new things about the government but it showcased to me how much mother was deeply invested in this scheme.

My mother's office was incredible to just say the least, if I wanted to describe the place, it was more than amazing, my desk was seated outside a particular door that read Emilia Schmidt in writing. I peered inside and to my amazement, I saw some historical paintings hung proportionally on her walls, her oak desk was clean and glowing from all spaces, and on the window hanging from the ceiling down to the floor behind her chair was the famous swastika symbol. Someone tapped me on my shoulder and I turned around to see another unknown man that I did not recognise at all, I drew back wondering what he was going to do but my mother came between us and introduced him to me. The man's name was Karl Wagner, he was a close associate who had been working under my mother for quite a while, he greeted me by stating that he was relieved to find another person working with them since the pressure will be less of a burden. Karl escorted me around the whole office place introducing me to colleagues and workers who were paid by my mother to do certain roles, like helping expand the German Reich not just in Germany but worldwide.

Sometimes they would get visits from Goebbels who would discuss matters to my mother in meetings not involving me. I had my own desk which meant I had a small room to myself stacked with papers and other material I had to get done before the end of the day.

Karl showed me what I had to do which included: organising folders that my mother needed for her meetings with the leaders, sorting out new material involving campaigns in different cities in Germany for Hitler's expansion, learning the ins and outs of new policies that will be decided and implemented for future purposes during meetings and much more. In the beginning, it was a pressure load for me but over the weeks I began to cope and get accustomed to how things operated around the office. Now it made sense to me why my mother always came home late; this is what she had to deal with every single day and I was now a part of it. Karl Wagner was giving me new documents concerning a known policy concerning the Jewish customs in the German communities, he left it on my desk and was about to head out. Karl Wagner was one mysterious man indeed, I do not know why but I just could not trust him as well as my mother could, there were things about him that did not sit well with me. A known example is the things he says to other colleagues about my mother when she was not present in the office on certain occasions, calling her out on how she is not fit to be controlling this office for years, and why she is so trusted by The Fuhrer, why Goebbels even bothers to waste time giving her information on certain political discussions. It was sickening, and even if he was joking around, I was not laughing at all, I had to restrain myself sometimes from knocking the man in his jaw, but because of his loyalty to my mother he remained consistent and dared never to say jokes like that whenever she was around. He just did not have the balls to do it.

Anyway, back to the documents.

As he was about leave my desk, Karl suddenly paused and asked me if I had any Jewish friends who had lost their jobs. To my sudden response of no, he sat down on the chair opposite while I was writing up a finished paper report and started babbling about his cousin who had worked in a baker's factory selling customers delicacies. That was until after the Nuremberg Laws occurred, she had been kicked out and fired from her role.

I was not even listening to what he was saying and even worse he had not noticed that I was not listening, it was not that I was being rude, I just did not care, right now I had to show no emotion because this was one of my acting roles. If I showed a little concern or sympathy for his cousin's circumstances then he could easily use it against me. Once Karl had finished talking, he examined me and asked if I was doing all right, I did not bother to respond so I gave him the signal to leave me be and he got the message. Out of the corner of my eye, I caught my mother putting down the telephone set and packing her bags before rushing to Karl's office and then coming into mine ordering us both to follow her. She explained to us that we were heading to a meeting ordered by The Fuhrer. I almost felt nauseous, did she just say including Adolf Hitler? If I were in charge, I would have refused but that was not the case, it was more than that, and it was important because all the meetings I attended so far were mostly involving the colleagues in this particular office. I wondered why I had to attend this meeting. I mean I only started this job a month ago. I nodded my head and packed my bag and then my mother told me to take the papers on my desk as well which I roughly stuffed inside before quickly closing my bag.

From what I knew about Hitler's office was that it was based in Berlin. I had some knowledge about it when I asked Marcus Rhinestone who knew a great deal, since my mother told him many things about Hitler's office when she visited. From what I was told the Reich Chancellery was the traditional name of the office of the Chancellor of Germany which was called Reichskanzler since 1878. The Chancellery's seat was selected and prepared in 1875 and was the former city palace of Prince Antoni Radziwiłł, who passed away in 1833, on Wilhelmstraße in Berlin. In the days of the Weimar Republic, the Chancellery was significantly enlarged by the construction of a Modern southern annex finished in 1930. In 1932 and 1933, while his nearby office on Wilhelmstraße No. 73 was renovated, the building also served as the residence of Reich President Paul von Hindenburg, where he appointed Adolf Hitler chancellor on 30 January 1933. The Hitler Cabinet held few meetings there. In 1935, the architects, Paul Troost and Leonhard Gall redesigned the interior as Hitler's domicile. They also added a large reception hall/ballroom and conservatory, officially known as the Festsaal mit Wintergarten in the garden area. The latter addition was unique because of the large cellar that led further one-and-a-half meters down to an air-raid shelter known as the Vorbunker. From the news mother received a couple of days ago, which I overheard in a meeting with Goebbels and another man who was wearing glasses and had a slightly stretched moustache, the place was almost ready for completion. Not only was I intrigued by this information I received from Marcus, but currently I never expected me of all people to be able to see it first-hand, it was petrifying, but looking at mother and Karl they appeared so relaxed and composed, I mean they had been there before. However, there was a concerning expression in Karl's eyes and I could feel the same energy as well, he may have been there a couple of times but Adolf Hitler was a force to be reckoned with and we both knew how intimidating he was.

CHAPTER 16

IT DID NOT MAKE ANY sense to me when we arrived there at Adolf Hitler's office, we had been told to wait in a room not far from the door and outside near us were military leaders and other important people all dressed with the swastika symbol attached on the crest of their uniform. They all seemed so calm, just talking among themselves. This had to be very important. I stared at my mother who appeared like her normal self but in her eyes, there was no life. Turning to Karl who was holding tight to his bag trying not to tremble, but his legs gave it away. I almost felt like laughing but I did not want to because bringing attention to myself was unnecessary. I was even shaking myself. Not only was this uncomfortable, I hardly recognised anyone here except Goebbels who was standing near the Fuhrer's door whispering some words to the man near him. I remembered him, he was in my mother's office, who was he? Tapping Karl who almost jumped in fright, glared at me warning for me not to do anything like that ever again. I ignored his insult and slyly pointed to the man in the glasses, he followed my finger and told me angrily to put my finger down. Asking him who he was, Karl hissed at me that he was ashamed that I did not know who the famous figure was. Apparently, his name was Heinrich Luitpold Himmler. My eyes widened, I remembered the name, it was back in 1935 when I heard Goebbels mention his name in my old headteacher's office room after that certain incident. A shiver ran up my spine, I heard stories about him, but I did not know whether to believe them, not because I did not want to have faith that they were false but because I knew how accurately true it was. The doors opened and everyone fell dead silent in the room as if we were about to attend a funeral, a man ushered all of us individually, I gulped when it was my turn, but I was ready.

As soon as we sat down, some individuals were standing, and I was worried at how they would perceive me, but no one was glancing in my direction. Maybe it was because they knew who I was. I was seated next to my mother who was as quiet as everyone else, there was a timidness in the atmosphere, there were two double doors on the right-hand side and they automatically opened. Without hesitation every single person sitting down stood up as quickly as they could and saluted saying the usual saying, I, of course, was never a fan of it but I had no choice, I was in the presence of the most powerful man in Germany. When Hitler came inside, he had not changed from the last time I saw him when I was a child, however, the coldness in his eyes was apparent, I shivered again, my mother gripped onto my hand and signalled me to calm down. I relaxed and tried not to quiver so no one scented any weakness from me, I was not going to jeopardise that right now, or ever. Adolf Hitler, The Fuhrer, the most powerful man in Germany, examined everyone closely from left to right and from right to left before sitting down in his massive chair. I now understood why people were intimidated whenever they were around him, it was the dark aura that came from him, I see why my father called him a devil. I did not know that Karl was still shaking, I was about to touch him and tell him to put his act together, but then my eyes locked in with The Fuhrer. Those dark eyes, were so hollow I did not know what I was staring at, I was struggling to take my eyes off his, it was like he was hypnotising me and it was not helping. Hitler put his hand up and Goebbels instantly stood up and began to end the silence by bringing up why we were here, it was the next words he said that brought me back to reality, Anti-Jewish Propaganda.

"As we are gathered here with the honours given to me by our mighty Fuhrer of discussing the major points of increasing our agenda for not just Germany but worldwide. So, let me begin our next phase, so we shall firstly begin with the beginning of concentration camps which will be designated camps built to incarcerate habitual criminals or anyone who is constantly rebelling against our Fuhrer through low-level tactics such as trying to gain political gain or social gain. Moreover, later on, next year, we do not know when but we will be building an exhibition with the assistance of our good friend Adolf Ziegler who as you know played a major part in the past in purging this country of this disgusting and degenerate art by incompetent artists, and thanks to him the country has become a better place. The reason we are building this exhibition is not only for the Fuhrer's interests but to expand our impact on art culture upon the world and in Germany, to the point, we leave a mark for future generations after us. That is all. But now we shall get to how to achieve this and what everyone's roles are to make this a reality."

A LOST SOUL: THE REVELATION

For the next two to three hours, Goebbels and other important officials including The Fuhrer himself opened up and gave out relevant points and addressed issues that needed to be avoided for these two goals to be fully in effect for next year. It was almost the end of the year and the passion in all who spoke gave me a weird sense of hope even though I knew this was all to push their anti-Semitic ideas on the world, yet I understood, it sounded odd. Once the session drew to a close, everyone began to leave all excited by what had been discussed in the room, no one was allowed to communicate with anyone else about it who was not designated to any role, but most people in the room knew not to. Hitler was not someone to play with, if he found out then it meant severe consequences and no one was trying to risk that, not now or till the end of time. My mother rose from her chair, and I followed suit, so did Karl who had calmed down compared to when we first arrived, it was until Goebbels confronted us and told us that Adolf Hitler wanted to see us before he left for other urgent matters. My mother greeted him, Karl was overdramatic, he was bowing down as if he were some sort of servant, and I could tell Hitler was amused. When his eyes laid on me, a shimmer glimmered in them, I offered my hand and he shook it roughly almost breaking my arm, it seemed like he remembered me. I tried hard to smile and laugh but it would not come out, then his face changed and he let go of my hand and ordered Goebbels that we needed to leave. He nodded at us and we were escorted by one of the soldiers out of Hitler's office and the soldier shut the doors loudly. That was a weird reunion but I was glad it was over, there were too many sudden experiences that occurred this past week that I did not want to go through again. Karl and my mother were already leaving the area and I was falling behind, I was still thinking about what was troubling The Fuhrer, I wanted to find out but at the same time I did not want to pay it no mind, that was his problem, not mine. It was a rude way of thinking but I was just being realistic, I did not like the man but I liked Goebbels, yet sometimes I questioned why I did, was it because he was nice to me? Maybe it was, but how did that affect me? If I was in his good graces, I would rather keep it that way.

CHAPTER 17

AFTER THE INTENSE MEETING, my mind went back to the dinner in 1930 when Hitler came to my house for the first time. It was a weird experience after I had escorted him to the door. Once I closed the door, I peeked out the window and caught him meeting up with a much larger man who was wearing a military uniform, and then he escorted Hitler inside the vehicle he came in. For some reason, I closed the curtains because I was worried the man next to him would look towards the window. I heard the car speed down the street and my heart calmed down, I felt relieved. I felt a tap on my shoulder and instantly shivered afraid that it was my mother next to me, but once I turned around to apologise, I found out it was my little sister, Mia, giggling and holding onto her mouth. Infuriated by her antics, I stormed off leaving her there confused for some hours, I did not want to explain anything to her, was she there during my conversation with Mr Hitler? I did not care, either way, all I wanted was to go back and finish my dinner, I had been so busy staring at the window that I did not realise my food was probably cold.

The radio was still on, and my grandmother was sitting in the living room relaxing on the sofa, I went to see what was wrong, but I then paused and smiled willingly, she was just sleeping. As I entered the dining room, there was no one at the table, I felt much better, Beatrice, our maid, came to clear the plates but she winked at me and left mine, seems like she read my mind, I winked back at her and proceeded back to eating. The food was bland compared to how it was when it was dished out, it tasted horrible but because Beatrice was still there waiting for me to finish, I swallowed down every piece to the final bite, I wiped the drool from my mouth and gave her the plate. Confused by my facial expression, she patted me softly on my head, I understood that it was for the best, Beatrice and father were the only people I trusted in the house, speaking of father I wondered if he was okay, I pushed my chair back and started searching for him.

Making my way up the stairs, I went through each door all down the hallway, he was not there, neither was mother or grandfather, were they all together or did they all go outside? I had to find out. Checking the guest room, I decided to find my father's notebook but it was not there, which I began to piece together that if it was not there it had to be in his study room. That was where they all were. Running down the steps and pushing Mia out the way, who I almost knocked into, I made my way towards the oak door, it was slightly open but I could hear shouting from the distance, it was my father. Sneaking near to the door, I put my ear against the oak surface, it sounded as if father and mother were arguing, they were discussing Mr Hitler, and why was father calling him a devil? Maybe he was just annoyed, is it because Mr Hitler did not like Jewish people? I was so intrigued by the conversation that I did not hear the cough behind me, I looked up and my eyes widened, it was grandmother, she had a dark expression on her face. I thought she was taking a nap on the sofa, but it seemed like I must have misinterpreted the display, had she been pretending? Grabbing my arm fiercely, she pushed open the door, and the light bounced off my eyes, I squinted and saw the horror in my father, mother and grandfather's faces. I did not know what to say, it was not my fault, then suddenly grandfather grabbed me tightly by the arms, and stared at me directly in my eyes with disgust, shouting at me and asking how much I had heard. I lied to him, I had to, I responded saying that I did not hear anything nor did I understand. Letting go of me, he went back to get his pipe and breathed out the fume of smoke that came out his mouth and nose. My grandmother was still beside me and it was then when my father who stared at me relaxed his expression even though in his eyes, I could see he was embarrassed, he escorted me outside. He told the three people in the room that he would be returning to discuss the issue further, but as I stood outside, he whispered some words to my mother. She nodded and looked at me before escorting my grandparents to another room. Deep down I had a feeling my mother knew that I had lied to my grandfather. That was why she had glanced at me like that. The look of embarrassment and shame. My father grabbed my hand and closed the door quietly, he stared at me and smiled but I did not give him the same response back, I could not, after what I had just heard, but I tried forcing a grin to get his approval. As we went upstairs, he called Mia who sprinted behind us. She seemed so lively compared to when Adolf Hitler had visited over twenty minutes ago. Staring at my father, I knew why he was taking us upstairs, it was time for both of us to go to bed, even though it was much earlier than usual, it was for our own good.

Before my father left my room, I called him to answer some questions that were playing on my mind, he whipped his head around shocked, but he eventually closed the door and went to sit next to me as I lay on my bed. I pulled the covers towards my face to get warmer, but inside I felt cold, I was worried about how my father would react to what I was about to say:

"Father, I have been meaning to tell you that I lied to grandfather..."

"I already know you lied, but it was good you did, I do not know what your grandfather would have done if he found out otherwise."

"Erm father, why do you not like Mr Hitler? I heard you call him a devil, why?"

"It is hard to explain son, but I do not trust that man, but that is just me, personally I do not like how he views Jewish people, that is all."

"Are you sure father? You looked incredibly angry."

"There is no need for you to worry, you are still a child, you should not be thinking about those types of things, what you should be focusing on is getting ready for school, okay?"

"Okay, I promise father."

"You know I love you no matter what happens Matthew, so just know that your mother, your grandfather and grandmother love you very much too."

"I know father."

"All right then, now that is all sorted, I will call Beatrice to read a story to help you get some sleep, goodnight son."

"Goodnight father."

Smiling at me, I noticed there was sadness in his eyes but I did not understand why. He quietly closed the door before uttering the words good night. I gazed up at the ceiling and thought about the conversation I heard from my whole family, if my father did not like Mr Hitler, I hope he could talk things out with him. What was I thinking? Just from the dinner we had, I knew the man was crazy. I did not know what my mother and grandfather saw in him, in my mind I was praying for everything in my household to get better. My father is right about one thing. I am too young to understand the situation he is in. I sighed. Maybe sleep is the best medicine for me right now. I wanted to forget everything that occurred, and wake up to a new day. The door unlocked and I heard the creak of the door become louder and louder. Turning my head, I smiled with tears rolling down my face. It was Beatrice and she was carrying a sleeping Mia while holding onto a bright red novel in her right hand, I was so glad.

"Matthew are you okay? Why are you crying? Did something bad happen?"

"No Beatrice, I am just glad you are here, but I do not know why."

Closing the door shut, she grabbed the wooden chair in my room and laid Mia next to me in my bed before tucking her in. Mia snuggled her face near my chest and held onto my hand, I held onto it even tighter. I could feel her soft, small fingers curl around my own. Beatrice sat down and began reading the book she was holding. It was a book she had bought herself at the store, and she had decided for us to hear it every time we went to sleep; it was all about a group of children in Germany who were discussing their experiences in the peaceful country they lived in. I tried to close my eyes but it would not shut, so I decided to stare at the wall until I fell asleep. This was all I needed, the only peaceful thing in the house, Mia and Beatrice were my favourite people, besides father, the only people that kept me sane in this cycle of madness. Deep down I could hear an eery voice warning me that things were not going to get better in this house but I had hope, I needed the hope because without it I knew that I was going to lose my mind, and I did not want anyone else to lose their minds either, especially Mia, she did not deserve any of this, I was going to protect her no matter what. Eventually, my eyes closed and the tiredness was settling in, the darkness was closing around me, and I allowed myself to be consumed. All I could see was black, nothing but black.

Opening my eyes, the first thing I saw was my father, he was holding my hand, we were in a field filled with trees and flowers. I felt confused about where we were but I still allowed my father to lead me to our destination. Suddenly, he paused and let go of my hand, and I tried to hold it but he was disappearing, my hand was just going through him, I began to cry not knowing why this was happening, I was just slipping through him like he was translucent. My father was fading away slowly, I tried grabbing him again and again but nothing was working and then like a ghost in the light he vanished into thin air. I fell to my knees wondering why this was all happening to me, the trees began to fade as well and so did the beautiful flowers that were dancing to the wind's rhythm, the light began to turn into golden orange and I could see the grass forming into a sandy peach format. An anonymous person was making their way towards me, I got up from the sand and began to sprint away not knowing what it was going to do to me, however, my feet were sinking in the sand, no, my whole body was sinking.

The mysterious man clicked his fingers instantly and the sand parted into two dropping me into a wilderness setting, there were no trees, no flowers, just a hot blazing sun and a pure, blue sky. I did not know if we were on terrain or if it was just an unknown land. The man stopped in front of me and grabbed me by the throat, I struggled to move as he lifted me slowly from the ground, from his grip I could tell he was extraordinarily strong. I gazed into his eyes while he gazed into mine, his eyes reminded me of my own, they had the same dark blue sea colour that I always stared at in the mirror every morning, his expression relaxed all of a sudden and he dropped me. Landing painfully on the floor, I glared at him but he did not seem to be bothered if I was hurt or not, he told me to follow him and tossed me a small knife. I did not bother to question where he found it, but I hurried up beside him so I would not get lost, wherever he was taking me could help me know where my father had disappeared to.

The sun was messing with my head, it was boiling and my clothes were soaked in sweat, I sniffed my armpits and turned away in disgust, the stench coming from my clothes was horrible. The man next to me was yet unbothered by me, it was as if I was not even there, I tried waving at him but it did not work, so I jumped in front of him, but he waltzed past me like a ghost. I was extremely terrified, was he my father in disguise? No, that was impossible, who was this person and why did he want me to tag along with him like I was some sort of lost puppy? The irony of it was I was lost and he was my only way of knowing how to adapt to where I was currently located, and if I did not go with him, someone else may take me hostage or even worse kill me. Shaking my head, I complained to him about why we were just walking constantly and if there was a destination, he stopped and turned in my direction before hissing at me to be quiet for the time being. I obeyed without hesitation and zipped my mouth shut; I did not want to end on this man's bad side, but yet again, I had the right to know where he was taking me. My answers were met when from the distance, I could see a rural town, it was small compared to the view, however the closer we got to it I realised how huge the town was. The place reminded me of the old-fashioned monuments I studied with father when my family went to Egypt.

Two guards decided to stop us with weapons, the man next to me raised his hands and showed he had nothing on him. The guards nodded and allowed him inside. One of the guards glared at me, but it took me a while to realise he was intrigued by my clothes. I decided to reveal to him that I had nothing on me either, he nodded and allowed me through. I thought about why they were holding spear-like knives; did they not have any guns? I found it weird. Suddenly, the man gripped my arm and pointed to an inn that was a distance away, I stared at him and agreed, he then dragged me to the front door without warning me. I thought about why we were staying in an inn, but I decided not to speak, he was familiar with this place more than I ever could. Inside was a small desk, around it was some candles laid near the counter, the man ordered me to sit on the stool next to the entrance, I gladly obliged and sat next to an old woman who was snoring loudly.

A LOST SOUL: THE REVELATION

The woman at the desk gave the man a small wooden board with random numbers engrailed on it, I could not see from the angle I was sitting, but if I noticed one of them read the number 45, the man whirled to face me and signalled for me to come with him whether I liked to or not. As we climbed the stairs, it frustrated me because the creaks were very loud, but it scared me at the same time. Sometimes I wondered if it would break. Once we reached the top, we went to the numbers that were on the board, my room was 45 and his number was 46, he gave me a key, and I saw him unlock his door and shut it loudly. I tried to do it but I failed miserably, a man from the next room opened his door yelling at me, I broke away and locked my door to avoid trouble. The room was different from my original bedroom, it was not luxurious or even appealing: the bed only contained a sheet and there was no pillow, the window was left open and there was a petite chair near the bed. I began questioning whether this was all a dream or if this was really reality. Where was Mia, Beatrice, my mother, and my grandparents? It made no sense. I was right next to Mia before I slept. Was this all an illusion? And if so, how could I wake from it?

CHAPTER 18

THE MEALS THEY SERVED us at our time in the inn were either bread, beans, cake, or rice, I didn't even know how long we would stay. We were both sitting on a wooden table that almost looked like it was about to fall apart because the wood was eroding and it kept shaking every time we began to eat. I coughed on purpose to get his attention and those dark blue eyes glared at me, I then asked him the question I kept within me for the past three days, it was worth it. The response he gave to me threw me off guard, he said that we only had a day left until we would make our way to a city called Jerusalem, I almost choked on my food.

Did he just say Jerusalem?!

That was impossible. How did I get from my bedroom in Berlin to Jerusalem? It did not make any sense. I instantly gripped onto his clothing not letting go; I was creating a scene since I did not notice everyone in the inn staring at me as if I were crazy or delusional. The man gripped my clothing and slowly picked me up before throwing me to the ground. I winced in pain and rubbed my back, there was a fury in his eyes and he grabbed me once again before picking me up and apologising to the people that were present. Dragging me back to his room, I ordered for him to let go, but he did not let go, I bit into his hand and he shouted out before releasing me, he took out a pistol and aimed at my head, his finger was on the trigger. The anger in his eyes was still there, but I was not afraid of him anymore, I grabbed the point and pressed it against my forehead glaring back at him waiting for the bullet to enter my brain. I closed my eyes and his finger tightened around the trigger but then he pushed me roughly away and put his weapon back into his pockets, I knew he could not do it, he huffed at me and trudged back to his room.

In the room he was staying in, I decided to stand next to the door in case he did anything unexpected, I was not fearful but alert and I was not afraid to fight back even if I knew he was much stronger, weighed more and was more muscular than me. Staring deep into my eyes, he breathed out and took out his weapon and left it on the table, he raised his hands and made sure he would not shoot. I carefully went to sit on his bed which did not bother him, I was starting to see maybe he was not as evil as he portrayed himself to be, I was glad.

"Where are my family members?"

"What are you talking about boy?"

"I mean my sister, my mother, my father, and my grandparents."

There was silence, he was silent, the windows flapped, the wind was calm, no one was speaking, I do not know what I said but it was like he knew some hidden secrets I didn't have a clue about.

"They are.... fine boy, you do not need to worry about them."

"Then who are you? You never told me your name."

"I......I cannot tell you that, but I will tell you that the time you are living in is not your time."

"What do you mean? Is the year not 1930?"

"I will be blunt with you boy, the year we are now in is 1955."

"Wait.... wait.... did you just say 1955? You must be joking......"

"From now on I want you to address me as M."

"Is that your actual name? Why am I in the future? What have you done with my family?"

"Save your questions for later, I will answer them as soon as we get to our destination, but until then you have to wait."

"Promise me you will tell me what is going on because I cannot trust you right now."

"It does not matter to me if you do not trust me, but my word is my word."

I rose from the bed and confronted him and raised my hand to shake his, he hesitated and then smirked, both our hands shook and I knew that the agreement was settled, I had to know what he was hiding from me by all means. This was more than something personal, my family could be in trouble, but he directly told me the year was 1955, which meant things had occurred in between the 25 years that passed. I was not going to give up. I did not know what to call this, I remember reading a book in school about "time-travel" which was not real but then again, I was witnessing it first-hand right now; it was going to be a long journey back home.

The next day we said goodbye to the innkeeper and started to hunt for a vehicle available to purchase because our destination to Jerusalem was too distant from here, we stumbled across a merchant who was leaning next to a dusty car that appeared to be still in use. The man was surrounded by different types of items from bells to old-fashioned pots. I pointed to the one vehicle and M smiled at me before straightening his jacket and approaching the man in front of the car.

"Excuse me, sir, how much is that vehicle you are leaning on?"

"Are you willing to buy this old piece of junk?"

"Well, do you have any other vehicles besides this one?"

"Yes, I do, but what do you need them for? Is that your child?"

"No, that is my erm......my nephew, he is just travelling with me for the time being."

"I understand, well, we have this one which I will get out.... hold on."

The man disappeared into a massive tent, the front entrance was flapping in the heat, I was sweating and hungry. Five minutes later, two younger men began to push another vehicle in our view. My eyes widened, the vehicle was much cleaner, the tires were like they had just been replaced, and the inside of the car including the seats were sparkling. Where did this man purchase or steal this car from? I had never seen a car like this, was this how cars were going to be in the future? It gave me a bright hope that the times ahead were going to be incredible. M nodded and shook the man's hand and went to his bag revealing a large number of money notes, he slapped it into the man's hand who seemed not only surprised but excited too. It must have been his first time seeing that amount of money, unlike me who didn't appear impressed. The amount this man had was nothing compared to what I had seen in grandfather's house. Both M and I went inside the car, M started the engine and the car sped off across the sandy terrain, we exited the gates and sped down the main road, I looked back to see the town now only a small black dot in a golden setting. The next destination was Jerusalem.

During our journey ride, I decided to have a conversation with M since not only did I want to break the awkward silence, but I wanted to get to know more about him even if he was going to tell me where my family were. I wanted to know his character, his demeanour, his past, what he likes, what he does not like, they were all necessary if we were going to be partners. I smiled to myself, it was the first time I had seen M smile and it appeared to be genuine, I could tell the tough persona he brought was something to guard against others he did not like. I just hoped I would not become one of those people he would despise. There were not many cars on the road, it was weird to me, there were words on passing boards written in strange writing, I had never seen it before, I wondered what it is was, I knew we were in Jerusalem, but what had happened through all these years? I wanted to know, but at the same time I did not want to know. Staring at M, he seemed so calm, I did not know if this was another act or not, but I noticed his hands trembling slightly, I wanted to touch him but I decided against it. I checked out the windows and saw the rocky pathways where the women and children whose clothes were torn and wrapped with scarfs stared at me with emptiness in their eyes. It was like the pain they had witnessed was stuck in their minds and there was nothing anyone could do; it piqued my interest in why everyone was so depressed and why sadness was haunting the children.

"Erm M, I wanted to ask you something."

"If you are so willingly intrigued by who I am and where I come from, you know you can ask me, I do not bite."

"Okay, so I can ask you anything? Anything?"

"Well, except the terms we agreed on when it comes to your family."

"I fully understand, so where were you born because you don't look like you were born here."

"I was born in Germany, in a city named Berlin, but that place has changed compared to back in the day."

"So, did you move to Israel because the lifestyle is much better here?"

"You could say that but to be honest with you Germany is doing well, the nice parts of it of course."

"Is your family with you or do you travel alone?"

"Oh, my family lives in America, it is a nice place, better than what the newspapers and media portray it to be, I have two daughters, my wife is my rock and support. That woman supports anything I do, but back to your question, I travel as much as I can. You could call this a holiday for me."

"So why is everyone in this country so depressed? It gives me the creeps."

"Well, I was not planning to tell you this but, a few years ago there was a war here in Jerusalem back in 1947 and it continued to the summer of 1948, it was disastrous. It was called the "Battle for Jerusalem", it occurred during the 1947–48 Civil War in Mandatory Palestine. The Jewish and Arab populations of Mandatory Palestine, and later the Israeli and Jordanian armies, fought for control of Jerusalem. It was a turning point in this country, especially even before that when the...."

"What happened before that? Tell me."

"I.... I cannot, all you need to know is that the world changed after that man tried to take over it."

"Which man? Whom are you referring to?"

"Never mind, you will find out soon enough, let me focus on the road please."

I knew the topic we were discussing had annoyed him, I wondered which man he was referring to when he mentioned that the world changed because of him, he must have either done good or evil. In his eyes, those blue eyes, I could see a sparkling sense of grief in them, something must have happened to him, or even worse many things must have changed his insight on how he viewed life. I tried to talk to him but the words I said were not reaching him, maybe because he did not want to hear a child try and comfort him or lecture him about life. Relaxing in my chair, I did not know how long the tension between us was going to continue, I wanted to get out of the car and flee to another country, back to Germany, I did not want to do anything reckless but the recklessness in me was about to come out. I was only thirteen years old and I had a life to live, yet I was in Israel with a man, that was as cold as ice, heading to the capital of the country to learn about where my family were.

CHAPTER 19

JERUSALEM, THE CITY that explained it all, the original home for the Jewish people. I remember my father telling me stories about what he had learnt from his parents. Jerusalem is the religious and historical epicentre of the world. A surreal and vibrant city, holy to Jews, Muslims, and Christians all around. It did not matter what people thought of the city but it was a paradise. Well, father was not wrong in a way. As we entered the city, Jerusalem was as unique and special as grandfather and grandmother had portrayed it out to be. According to M, beyond religious and historic significance, Jerusalem is still building and expanding, currently revealing the capital of modern-day Israel and an advanced, dynamic city. I could see it, the buildings and roads, and the places that were being built higher. They were replacing all of these crumbling buildings and making sure that each building is put to use. The builders were doing a great job because the improvement was showcasing results. My father showed my mother, me and my sister a picture of how old Jerusalem used to be back in the past where my great-grandfathers lived, it was full of the historic and religious elements that make the city so special. The one-square-kilometre walled area is central to Judaism,

Islam, and Christianity. The Western Wall, in the Jewish Quarter, the last remaining wall of the Jewish Temple compound, is the holiest site in Judaism. Jesus died, was buried and resurrected in Jerusalem, and the Church of the Sepulchre in the Old City is shared between many denominations. In Islam, Jerusalem is said to be from where Muhammad rose into the heavens, and the Dome of the Rock makes this city the third holiest for Muslims. The four quarters of the Old City, Jewish, Muslim, Christian, and Armenian, each contrast with each other, yet what remains bizarrely constant is how the residents of this surreal place rush about on their daily business.

Now in this time, the modern Jerusalem is the capital of modern-day Israel containing the modern-day functions you would expect of any capital city. It amazed me, no, in fact, it astounded both of us. Although not as liberal as Tel Aviv which was just 45 minutes by road, Jerusalem has become a distinguished cultural centre for all people and there was much more coming according to M. The wave of the great food we tried when we arrived swept across Israel stemming from the deep roots not missed by the city, and there are some great places to relax in Jerusalem especially in the German Colony and along Emek Refaim Street, which is a bit of an oasis of modernity among this conservative city. Likewise, modern Jerusalem contains the shops and institutions you would expect anywhere else, as we travelled inwards and outwards from street to street, I noticed that some buildings were taken in much more care and consideration than others. All this, however, with a slight twist, as all buildings in the city, by law, contain the magical golden Jerusalem stone the city is well known for. When I was told this by M I almost did not believe him, but he whispered saying that the times compared to back then have escalated and changed not just for Jerusalem but Israel as a whole.

To my amazement, I discovered that there were fascinating arrays of museums in Jerusalem, some of which complete a visit to the city. While visiting them, M informed me of the most important one that was an asset to the city, it was called Yad Vashem, situated on beautiful Mount Herzl, this was Israel's memorial and place of commemoration for the millions who perished. However, when I asked him why they were remembering or honouring these Jewish people, he did not bother to answer my question. It must have been something he experienced or heard about in the past that deeply affected him mentally. The museum had been built in 1953, just two years ago, the appearance was stunning but I could tell the expansion of this museum was going to be built over time. The incredible museum had certain stories of brave Jewish civilians who died; however, M would make me avoid certain categories giving the excuse that these specific stories were not suitable for a child like me to read. I wondered what he was hiding from me. Along the way, the museum had chilling architecture and moving multimedia displays, overall, I got bored half-way through the journey because I was not intrigued by the whole layout in terms of walking, sometimes I felt like why we bothered to come here, but M told me that it was important to remember those who had fallen.

What was he blabbering on about?

Down the road from Yad Vashem, builders were establishing new houses with a huge selection of artistic, archaeological, historical and cultural displays. And in

Jerusalem is the Jerusalem Biblical Zoo, technically Israel's most popular visitor attraction with a great selection of animals which include animals from the Bible making it a playful theme for the children. Ultimately from what I could view and have visited, Jerusalem was like nowhere else, a city where old and new jostles for space, along with the three religions who call this city holy. Incredibly intense, Jerusalem, is somewhere beyond explanation, and no visit to Jerusalem could compare to anywhere I had been, no matter how long, I was glad M took me here.

All I needed to know now was where my family were in Jerusalem like M stated to me back in the inn, but something kept playing in my mind warning me that he was lying to me. At first, I kept ignoring the thought but after the days began to roll by, I kept questioning if he was keeping true to his word, to the deal that we made, the agreement that determined my life's future. Due to our vehicle's engine, we decided to get it checked by any mechanics nearby who were experts in that particular field. My mind was more focused on searching where my parents were, I tugged at M's jacket and asked him how long we had until I could see my family. Ignoring my question, M pushed me away and told me to sit down on the bench positioned outside the shop. The man fixing our car questioned M asking if there was problem between M and I, but M responded casually stating that there was no issue. The man felt more relaxed and resumed back to his work while M eyed me from the inside area watching me like a hawk, I understood why he was so frustrated but so was I.

Waiting for an answer was tiring because I wanted to see Beatrice, Mia, mother, father and my grandparents really badly.

A LOST SOUL: THE REVELATION

A few hours passed and the heat outside was melting me like a frozen icicle ready to melt, the climate was boiling and I had to take off my top to allow my skin to breathe, the sweat on my forehead fell like raindrops down my cheeks, my upper and lower body felt sweaty as well, not to mention the constant thirst for water crawling slowly into my mind. The heat, the city, M, everything around me was annoying me. I stood up from the bench contemplating about what I was going to do.

I could not take it anymore.

Rushing inside the shop, I gripped M who had fallen asleep, he woke up suddenly, almost falling out of his chair, and glared at me before ordering me to get back outside, but I was not listening to him, not this time. I started to raise my voice demanding where my family was and why it was taking so long to find them, the workers inside were giving each other worried looks wondering if M had abducted me. M tried to calm my temper down, but he knew that the more I questioned him, the worse the scenario was playing out for him. Gripping tightly to my arm he sprinted outside while dragging me along, he let go of my hand and abruptly struck me in my face, I was so stunned that I did not even feel it.

"Listen to me very well, I do not know where your parents are and I do not care."

"What do you mean? You said when we arrived in Jerusalem, we would find my family!!"

"Well, I lied boy, I do not know where your parents are or your sister or this Beatrice or your grandparents."

"So why did you take me with you?! What have I been doing all this time following your lead?!"

"I am a sorry boy, I do not know what you want me to tell you, yes I lied but it was for your own good."

"What do you mean it was for my own good?"

"To tell you the truth, if I had to tell or figure out where they are, most are probably in their graves."

"Wait.... what......what did you just say?!!"

"DID YOU NOT HEAR ME, CHILD? YOUR FAMILY ARE PROBABLY DEAD!"

I did not know if he was joking or not but I did not find it amusing, it was far from it, it was like the words had pierced deep into my heart. It hurt like hell. I backed away from him and did not realise the tears rolling down my face, I rushed towards M and flung my fists in his direction but he blocked it and shoved me back. I tripped and stumbled to the sandy surface. Getting up again, I tried to hit him, yet he moved out the way, I whipped myself around and started to throw my fists at him again, but he whizzed past me with ease. My lazy punches were not landing on him and it caused my rage to rise, I was like a crazy beast trying to sink its teeth in the prey's neck but it was hopeless, M blocked my next punch and grabbed it before squeezing tight. Those eyes, they angered me, I screamed and kicked him in the leg but it did not appear to be effective, he released his grip and I ran the opposite direction never looking back at him again.

Never will I allow him to see my face again.

The man had lied to my face, telling me my family were safe and sound, sympathising with me, befriending me, but it was all a lie, everything was a lie and my trust in him had vanished completely. I did not want to see his smug face again, how could you do this to me? Why would you state to me that you knew my parents were alive and breathing when they were dead?

Is this what would happen to them in the future?

I wiped my tears and headed down the street almost knocking over one of the rice pots near a seller's shop, he scowled at me and told me to be more careful, I apologised and continued to run. There was no way my parents, Mia or Beatrice were dead, it was impossible, I would find them myself, I had no choice but to do that, it was my only way of knowing.

I arrived back at the inn we were staying in Jerusalem, and asked the man at the desk if he heard of a man and woman that went by the last name Schmidt, he paused at what he was doing and asked me to repeat what I had just said. The smile in my face curled, and I repeated my question, but his expression darkened and he glared at me with abhorrence which caused me to shudder. The reply he gave unsettled my nerves, he told me:

"Oh, THAT woman, no, she died a long time ago, and I am glad she and her Nazi friends are all dead."

Why would he talk about my mother like that? And what did he mean by Nazi friends? The tears this time did not run down my cheeks, I felt empty, I nodded at him forcing a smile in which he just kept glaring at me before waltzing away. Trudging up the stairs I thought about what M had shouted at me prior, so if my mother was dead that meant....

I grabbed my head and tried pulling my blonde curls from my scalp. But I stopped. The tears were coming again. I tried to wipe them away, but they kept on flowing down my rosy cheeks. Raising my head upwards, something in me snapped. I fell to the floor and wept.

Why was this happening to me?

CHAPTER 20

THE THOUGHT OF MY PARENTS' dead hurt me like hell. I did not know how to process my feelings. Not only was the man disgusted by my question he said he was glad my mother was gone. I tried to erase the conversation but I did not have the strength to do it, I wondered if my family had done something horrible in the past for people like him to say that. I needed answers immediately. Someone knocked on my door but I was in no mood to see anyone right now. The person began to knock even louder so I eventually unlocked it. Standing at the entrance was a worried M drenched in sweat. Allowing him in, he strolled inside my room and went to sit down on the spare chair seated near the window frame, from the look on his face I decided that he was not only tired but his search for me must have taken hours. Joining him in the room, I positioned myself opposite him on another chair and kept scowling until his eyes caught my gaze; he knew what he had said before affected him and I did not know if he was here to apologise or just lecture me, but I was fully prepared. His lips were beginning to tremble and I noticed that he was coughing regularly, he then bowed his head and I heard one word that caught my attention:

Sorry.

I did not think in a million years this man would lower his ego to apologise to me. Usually, he would have shouted or yelled, but this time there was a change of heart and it left me perplexed. I pretended not to hear it and, on the outside, I shrugged it off but, on the inside, I was smiling. I did not want to show him my true feelings because I knew he would make fun of me. Staring into his eyes I could tell it was a genuine apology and I nodded at him indicating that I had accepted it. Forgiving was better than holding a grudge. That was what my father spoke about every day. However, I still had some troubling questions that needed to be answered, and I was not going to miss this opportunity.

"M, I want to ask you a very serious question, when you said about my family being dead, did you mean that?"

"Yes, I would not lie to you boy, I......I felt bad not telling you the truth from the start."

"I heard the innkeeper said he was glad my mother was dead, I want to know the truth, what did she do?"

M got up from his chair, this time the coughing had stopped, his face had become serious now, he stared at me and swerved his chair backwards and sat back on it without saying a word. Those ocean eyes were signalling to me if I was ready to hear all of this, if I was ready to consume the words that would come out of his mouth this very second. I was ready, more than ready. I nodded and he proceeded:

"As I said to you way back then, you have come to the future from the past, from the 1930s, right now you are in the mid-1950s, there was something your mother, Emilia Schmidt had done in the past that ultimately resulted in her death."

"What was my mother involved in?"

"Emilia Schmidt was associated with a party known as the Nazis, they were a group of people who had managed to achieve power in the early 1930s led by a man your family invested heavily into, Adolf Hitler."

"Wait......did you just say, Mr Hitler?"

"Yes, you first met in 1930, wait.... How old are you child?"

"I am thirteen years old."

"So, I was correct, I thought I made a mistake then.... phew, yes, he came to your house back in 1930 and your mother and grandfather invested into him financially helping him boost his popularity and interests, besides his famous book he wrote five years prior."

"How do you even know all of this?"

"The man was responsible for the slaughter of millions of Jewish civilians from the time he became Fuhrer to his death. That devilish man was responsible for another war that caused millions of people in the world to die, and your mother was deeply involved and supported his ideas as long as she was in power, as long as she had her position."

The rage in his eyes was showcasing all around him, it was like some powerful aura was swirling, this was more than he could handle, the more he spoke about the matter, the more his feelings became apparent. I did not know what to say. My mother was involved in a scheme that resulted in Jewish people dying? I did not understand why this was so important to him, but it dawned on me that this was what had occurred during the 25 years. And what about father? Did he follow suit and get involved too? Everything M was saying was hurting my head, there was a ringing sound that was getting louder and louder, it was giving me a headache.

"Are you listening to me?!"

"Yes......yes, I am listening......but how do you know all of this? The detail you are giving sounds so precise as if you were present. Especially the details about Hitler visiting my home, the only people who were present were my grandmother, my grandfather, my mother, my father, Mia, Beatrice and me. So how is that even possible for you to know that? Tell me, please."

M rose from the chair and trudged towards me, his eyes were gazing down at me, sympathy and torment were shining from him to me, I froze not knowing what to do. What was he about to say? I closed my eyes waiting for him to strike me or hit me but both his hands rested on my shoulders. My eyes widened, tears were dropping to the floor, but they were not mine, they were his. The poor man was crying, but he was not making any noise, he did not wail, but he just stood there looming over me. Something inside of me felt heartbroken, I wanted to know what he was going through but at the same time, I would never understand.

"The reason I know so much about this, about your mother, about Adolf Hitler coming to your house in 1930, about everything your mother was doing is because I am her son, Matthew Schmidt."

The two last words echoed like a tunnel deep into my system, did he just say his name was Matthew Schmidt? That was my name, he had my name, no, he was me, I was him, we were both each other. I stepped backed almost falling from my chair, the pieces were starting to come together: the reason he wanted me to call him M, him ignoring my question on

A LOST SOUL: THE REVELATION

Mia and Beatrice, him making me avoid certain areas in Yad Vashem Museum, the way he kept treating me, but most importantly it was his eyes. Those deep, blue ocean eyes. How had I not figured it out? My breathing began to get heavier; my heart was beating much faster, I grabbed onto my chest confused why I was struggling to breathe. Maybe it was the information I received, maybe it was because my future self was standing right in front of me, maybe it was because I was fearful of what mother was going to do if I did return to the time I was living in, I just could not process everything as well as I wanted. My brain was falling apart like a puzzle that had just been scattered on the floor, the dizziness was settling in, for a brief moment I could see my whole family standing around me grabbing onto me and asking if I was okay, I was just hallucinating. No, this was no hallucination, what was this? Was it the heat? The chair leg broke and I fell roughly to the floor, M tried to assist me but I pushed him away, I was angry but yet nauseous, I suddenly puked allowing the food I had just eaten to pour out on the ground in a yellow puddle. The yellow liquid was dripping from my lips and I could feel the food rising again, I threw up again, but this time there was a mixture of red liquid. I touched my lips and examined it on my finger.

Was this blood? What was happening to me?

M was screaming and yelling for help, he told me to wait in the room before pelting out the door slamming it while I laid there lost in thought. I did not want to die. Not now. I had too many things I wanted to do in my lifetime. The funny thing was that I had already met how my future self-acted, I should have just asked him what I had achieved. Two men came in with M and they tried asking me if I was okay, I could not even hear them, my eyes were losing sight, they all seemed so blurry, the darkness was consuming me. All I could see was darkness. Nothing else. I was in darkness.

"MATTHEW......"

"Matthew......is he okay?"

"I do not know, but he has been out of it for a few days now......"

"Matthew.........please wake up.........my son......"

"What if he never wakes up? The doctor is not even sure...."

"Do not say that! Have some faith........."

Everything around me went quiet all of a sudden, first, it was the voices, then I could hear someone trying to talk to me, and now it is so quiet. Utter silence. Where was I? Ah yes, I was in Israel, Jerusalem with......someone, no, I was with my future self, Matthew Schmidt. I squinted my eyes and all I could see was a creamy ceiling, I examined my surroundings as soon as I whipped my head both left and right, I was on a bed, but it was not mine, wait, no this was my bed.

What year was this?

I noticed a woman sitting there reading a newspaper, the bright light was blocking my view so all I saw was blonde hair, her face was blurry to me. The woman stopped reading and changed her view before checking herself with a man dressed in all white that was standing near the bedroom door. Nodding at the woman, the man eventually opened the door and went out before closing it shut, I tried to sit up but my head was still pounding. The woman got much closer and I realised it was my mother, Emilia Schmidt, she hugged me and I hugged her back, but then instantly flashbacks came of M shouting at me, what he mentioned about mother and what she was going to do, I instantly pushed her away and threw the covers over my head. At the corner of my eye through the bedsheets, I could see mother's shadow shaking her head and then waltzing towards the door before heading out herself. When she had gone, I pulled the covers from my face and examined the ceiling wall, and that was when the doctor opened the door again, I could now see how he looked like; he was wearing a white suit with the swastika on his middle section, he was buttoned up and wearing black gloves, his hair was slicked back and he was wearing oval-shaped glasses. Assisting me in sitting up on my bed, he went to drag a chair from the other room to mine before side-eyeing me up and down, he must have had some questions but I had some of my own but if it was a game he wanted to play, so be it.

"Erm, Matthew, can I call you Matthew?"

"Yes, you may."

"If you are not aware of your surroundings you are in your room, and to be quite frank with you, you have been unconscious for almost five days."

"Wait.... five days?!! What year is this?"

"Why are you asking? Have you forgotten the year you are in? You are very funny indeed; the year is 1936."

"Oh yes, I knew that I just woke up and was feeling very peculiar so I needed to double-check."

"If you need a backstory of why you are here it is because your mother stated you fell abruptly from walking down the stairs on your way back from The Fuhrer's main office. Luckily even though you hit your head on the last step which knocked you out completely, there weren't any major injuries involving your brain, no need to stitch anything that you need to be concerned about."

"I do remember coming from the stairs, I was not myself I was thinking back to a time in the past."

"May I ask what that was if you do not mind?"

"It was when The Fuhrer had visited my house back in 1930, almost six years ago now."

"I see, well, at least I know, did anything else unusual happen before you fell."

"Nothing that I can remember."

"Okay, thank you for being cooperative with me Matthew, you still need to rest even if you have just awoken from your "slumber". And do not worry about the work you have missed; your mother has agreed to make sure the work you were supposed to complete will be sorted out by her assistant Karl. Now, let me leave to rest and if you need anything from your mother, she told me to tell you to ring this bell on your desk and your maid will come to your aid as quickly as she can."

"Is my sister all, right?"

"Yes, she was the most worried, she visited your room yesterday, right now the only people in this house are your mother, your maid and I, and of course you. Your sister must supposedly be at school, so do not worry; I need to head out now since I have other patients as well, but I will come to visit you tomorrow to check how you are doing. Good-bye Matthew and try not to do anything that will hurt you."

"Thank you so much, doctor."

Once the doctor reached the door handle, he turned back to me and said:

"This was settling on my conscience, but Matthew please try to not get caught up in trouble. I have heard a few stories about you in past discussions and I feel that you deserve much better."

Surprised by this comment, I zipped my lips and crossed my heart signalling that I would not, he beamed at me before leaving and shutting the door, I heard the key twist and I relaxed finally knowing I was all by myself again.

CHAPTER 21

MY RECOVERY OVER THE next couple of days started to change, I noticed my body and mind were adjusting back to how things were before the incident occurred, but what always kept playing at the back of my mind was the dream I had, or if it was an illusion or not. For some reason, before I went to sleep, I tried to go back to that time, but my eyes opened and I rose breathing heavily and sweating. There were days when sleep was not the best for me, it caused me to be fearful of never being able to wake up ever again, I did not want that to happen. Then there were days where I would hear noises in the dark, I would cover myself and roll up into my covers waiting for someone outside to try and force the door open. It was no mess but it was torture, I could hear someone calling my name regularly and the more I heard it, the more I realised it sounded just like M. I called back to him but he would not respond. I hated it here, in this country, I did, and it was all because I now knew what was going to happen in the future. But they say that what you know is going to happen can be avoided.

How could that be avoided?

I did not have control over this country, I was not Hitler, I was not Goebbels, I was not even my mother, yet I could not allow this to occur. Even though I knew realistically I had no power to stop it. Beatrice should not die, neither should Mia, neither should mother, and father was already gone because of her, even if I was still searching for clues to prove it, deep down I knew mother had her hands completely dirty in this. There was a sudden tap on the door, and I rushed back into my bed pretending to sleep, the key unlocked and someone came inside, the footsteps got closer and closer towards the bed and then I felt their warm hands caressing my face. I did not want to do anything because they probably thought I was sleeping soundly and did not want to wake me up, from the touch I knew it was a woman, but who was it? I slyly turned around to the other side facing them with my eyes still shut, their hands were not caressing my face anymore, that was odd, had I given myself away? Did they realise I had been awake this whole time? Before I knew what was going on, I could feel their lips touching mine, my eyes instantly widened and I almost fell off the bed, what the hell was this person trying to accomplish?! Once I saw who it was, I sighed and just sat there not knowing what to say. The person who had tried to kiss me was none other than Lulu. Louise Rhinestone.

Not only was I shocked that this woman was in my room, but I was also confused. How had she managed to get into the house? it did not make any sense. The last time she was in this house, my sister, Beatrice and I almost got killed; what the hell was going on? I was still on the floor staring deeply into her eyes, she seemed glad to see me and I was not ready to risk anything yet, not yet, I eyed the half-opened door and wondered if I was the only person at home. It would make perfect sense if that were the case, but then how would she be able to get inside if our key were locked from the inside? How did she even unlock my bedroom door? There were so many questions that were racketing up in my brain, none of it was adding up, I needed to picture the possibilities, no, I had to find a way past her and get some help. However, first I had to stabilize a conversation with her to get things going, get her off guard and sprint towards the door. That was the plan.

"Lulu, how did you even get inside my house?"

"Why do you ask? Are you not happy to see me?"

"Yes....and no, I am recovering from an accident so you waltzing into my room unexpectedly scares me."

"I understand, I just knocked on the door and Beatrice allowed me inside."

"Are you certain? The last time you came here Beatrice did not really "allow" you in this house, did she? Speaking of Beatrice, where is she right now?"

"Oh, she is in your living room sleeping on the sofa, she is very tired."

"Is there anyone else in the house?"

"No, I was just invited inside by Beatrice and asked her where you were and she told me you were sleeping upstairs, so I came up to see how you were doing."

I knew something fishy was going on, maybe trying to get her off guard is the wrong decision, I have to think of an excuse to leave the door, there is no telling what she has in her bag, probably a weapon.

"Well, if you would kindly excuse me, but I have to use the toilet, I am not feeling so well."

"That is fine, I can come with you if you want me to."

"No, that will not be necessary Lulu, I can handle myself, remember I am not a child."

Rising from the floor, I forced a convincing smile and she beamed back at me without hesitation, it reminded me of those creepy but innocent smiles you would see in a horror film. I gulped loudly before walking normally to the door. As soon as I got past the door, I told her to wait in my room, and give me fifteen minutes before I would return, that would be enough for me to figure out what was going on. Shutting the door, I went towards the toilet and pretended to go inside before loudly shutting it. I sighed to myself before making my downstairs carefully. Once I got to the entrance hall, I sneaked into the living room and noticed Beatrice on the couch sleeping, so Lulu was right, I scratched my head confused.

Did Beatrice really let her inside the house?

I decided to return upstairs until at the corner of my eye I noticed one of the picture frames was broken, I picked it up and examined it, there were small red dots visible on the golden frame corner. Trailing myself back to Beatrice, my eyes popped out when I caught a large red bruise angrily glaring at me, her arm was bruised as well, I touched it and felt the lump was recent.

Did they get into a fight?

One thing was certain, Lulu had knocked Beatrice unconscious and she placed her there. I instantly began to panic. I needed to call the doctor, anybody, I searched for bandages in the kitchen and started digging into each cupboard. Where were they? That was until I reached the final drawer and I saw the box sitting there on the top, I grabbed it and made my way back to the living room and then paused.

Right in front of me was Lulu, she did not appear to be impressed with my antics and had caught onto my lie. The only issue was that my path to Beatrice was blocked.

Beatrice was still slumped on the sofa; I was in the living room gripping tightly to the bandage box and Lulu was opposite me near the entrance door pointing a pistol at me. My legs were shaking, my arms were shaking, every part of my body was shaking, this was not only unexpected because I didn't even see or hear her coming downstairs, but my theory about her holding a weapon was far from wrong. It was a different pistol compared to the last time she was here, and what frightened me the most was that her finger was curled around the trigger. The woman was ready to shoot me down, if necessary, her eyes showcased that, I raised the bandage box and signalled to her I had to use it to treat Beatrice. Sighing at me, Lulu ordered me to pass her the bandage box, I hesitated at first, but she raised her pistol and shot at the ceiling creating a loud bang. I passed her the box and went back to my original position. Smiling cunningly at me, she took the bandage box and opened one of the windows before throwing it outside, I stared at her in horror, I wanted to stop her, but she had the upper hand. Lulu then told me to come and stand beside her, I did not even bother to refuse, I slowly walked towards her and stopped as soon as I got close to her face. Staring up at me, she frowned and then abruptly struck me with the gun in my face, I stumbled back falling to the floor, I touched my nose which was bleeding, what was her problem? Gripping me roughly by my collar, she pulled me up and sat me on the sofa, I tried to get up but she pressed the gun tightly to my forehead, I raised my hands before resuming back into the chair. I did not know what she wanted. Without indicating to me what she was about to do, she sat on my lap facing me before gazing deep into my eyes, the gun was now pressed against my chest, I was so worried for my life that I did not bother to react or move in case she shot me. Lulu pressed her lips against mine and she started to kiss me passionately, I was thrown off guard. She then slipped her tongue into my mouth before biting deeply on my lip. I pushed her back grabbing onto the lip and wiping my mouth, there was blood spread across my hand, I touched my lip with my finger and stared at the crimson colour floating on my skin. I glared at her but she just pressed the gun to my chest even harder. There was one thing that had not changed.

She was still a fucking psychopath.

The predicament of this scenario was out of my control, Beatrice was unconscious, my mother was at work, my sister was in school, and I was being forced against my will by Lulu. The woman had kissed me then bit my lip for no particular reason, and now she was still on my lap but this time she was unbuttoning my pyjamas, I tried to pull her off me but I decided against it, the gun was still pressed to my chest. As she continued to unbutton my clothes, I gaped around for anything within reach I could use for self-defence, from the books to the ball laid next to the chair, I had to figure out a strategy to get out of this nonsense. Lulu grabbed my face with her other hand and twisted to face me, she looked annoyed, was it because I was not focusing on her? I bowed my head low and in dismay, I realised she was on the last button, she then got off my lap and was standing on the carpet with the pistol pointing directly at me, her eyes had changed, they looked empty. I tried to sit up but she ordered me to stay where I was,

I had no clue what was about to happen but I was not looking forward to it.

"Matthew, listen to me very carefully, I want you to take off your pyjamas, I have done you the pleasure of unbuttoning the top for you."

"But why? What is the...."

"I SAID TAKE OFF YOUR PAJAMAS."

Afraid of what was going to happen if I did not listen, I obediently took off the pyjama she unbuttoned carefully before throwing it furiously onto the carpet floor. There was now a glimmer in her eyes, she was enjoying this very much, it made me sick, I wanted to just run and leave.

"Good, now I want you to take off your pyjama pants, and I want all of it taken off, the only thing I want on your body is your boxer trunks."

"Are you serious? You are sick in the head; you know that right?"

"I did know that Matthew, now do what I have told you to do or else...."

"Ok, ok, fine I will do it, do not rush me."

I slipped off my pyjama pants and rolled them into a ball, I threw it again on the floor filled with anger and rage, she was testing my patience. All I had on was my boxer trunks, everything else was gone, Lulu whistled at my physical appearance, there was a slight drip of drool leaking from the corner of her mouth, I was disgusted. Waltzing towards me still waving the pistol at me, she started to caress my chest and then she used her finger to trail like a snail making its way home slowly down to my abs area. I tried not to squeal or fight because I was feeling ticklish. This was wrong in so many ways.

A LOST SOUL: THE REVELATION

Lulu laid the gun against my leg before picking it up again and using it to trail down my back, she was using both the gun and her hand to touch me in different places, and I did not like it one bit. All of sudden, she pushed me forcibly onto the chair and told me to lay down warning me that if I were to try to reach for the gun, she would shoot me. I did not even listen to her words, I was more fearful of what she was about to do to me, was she going to hit me or even scratch me? I was sweating and my hands were trembling, all I could do was pray that my sister would get home as quickly as possible, I was the prey and Lulu was the predator, she was hungry and I was her main dish.

Closing my eyes, I waited for the worst, but then I felt something wet on my body, I opened my eyes and to my shock, Lulu was licking my chest. I could not even move, not because I did not want to, but because it was impossible, she was on top of me licking on my chest and abs, I began to blush closing my eyes not knowing where this would to lead to but deep down, I knew what was going on. From the far corner of the chair, I saw the pistol lying there, it was within reach but I remembered what Lulu said about if I tried to reach for it, she would kill me, I had to be cautious and just sneakily pull the gun carefully next to me. As she continued stroking my body and licking me, my hand moved silently towards the gun, she paused and went to lick my neck, I froze, she went from my neck to my face and began to nibble at my chin, I waited until she proceeded back to my chest before moving my hand again, I felt relieved. This was going to be difficult, but as long as I focused on getting the pistol, I would eventually have the advantage. I just had to be patient.

CHAPTER 22

THE TIME WAS ALMOST past 3:00 pm, it would be around an hour until Mia would come back home but I was fearful that if she walked in on Lulu and I, she would not pick up on what was going on. Relying on her would be a disadvantage, I was not going to wait that long, I did not have time, Beatrice was in critical condition and needed my assistance but currently, that was impossible. Lulu was staring into my eyes indicating to me that she was enjoying this more than she should, I forced a smile while my hand was scurrying to find the pistol, I pretended to face Beatrice till I noticed the pistol was only an inch away from my needy fingers. Then all of sudden I felt my fingers slipping away from the weapon, it was not the pistol running away, it was me, I whipped my head back to face Lulu, she was dragging me down while I tried to pull myself up. I gripped onto the chair and caught her trying to slip down my boxer trunks, I knew where this was going, she paused and crawled up towards me and whispered something in my ear.

My eyes widened and I turned to face her in horror, my mouth could not even fathom what she had said, I nodded dutifully as she slipped herself back to my pants, I closed my eyes and that was when I felt it. I bit my lip trying not to drift away to the lustful place, I was prickling red, but my mind was telling me to focus on the pistol, my hands finally felt the cold metal and I gripped onto it before pulling it across the sofa towards me. Whatever she was doing felt incredible, but I was not going to allow that to stop me from reaching my goal, I hid the pistol behind my back avoiding her from getting an angle to see it from her position. Instantly I pressed the pistol on her head, and she stopped doing what she was doing, I hissed at her to let go of my private parts which she slowly did, cautiously. I slid warily across the couch allowing her to get up still pressing the gun against her head. Ordering her to sit across the chair, I stood up and pulled up my boxers, I then faced Beatrice to see if she was okay, she was still bleeding, but the blood had already dried up. Glaring at Lulu, I turned around to check on her condition, she had to get treatment quickly, waiting would not be good for any of us, and that was when I heard a clicking noise behind me. I dreaded the worst and whipped around to see Lulu with another gun in her hand, her demeanour had gone sour and she was angry at me. I did not know if it was because I had put a gun to her head or she did not get to finish her job.

There was no way in hell I was going to lower the gun, we both had weapons and I was waiting when she was going to shoot, I gripped my pistol and pretended to fire, Lulu did not notice the bluff and she pulled the trigger first. I hid behind the table as the bullet whizzed past the chair, I pushed the chair down and checked if Beatrice was all right, I sighed, the bullet had not hit her. Lulu shot again at me but missed and hit the window, tears were going down her eyes, but I still did not know why, I crawled beside the next chair and tried to reach for Beatrice but drew back my hand when a bullet flew past. This was not a warzone, but if I did not move quickly and communicate with her then it was going to be. I knew that Lulu was aiming recklessly, she was not focusing on me, but allowing her emotions to take over. This was a great advantage, if I could use that against her, I could get the upper hand, I squinted to see a reflection of Lulu from the mirror opposite, she was trying to find where I was hiding. I crawled slowly to see if she was still moving. I smiled to myself. She was still in her position. I crawled to the next chair, my goal was to get as close behind her as possible, I knocked one of the vases to the floor and it made a loud crash as the glass shattered on the floor. Lulu fired at the broken vase twice, I crawled once again to the chair facing behind her, she had not even taken a step forward yet; this was my time, it was now or never. I stood up and pointed the gun at her and yelled at her to drop her weapon, she whipped herself around and ignored my words before firing at me, I ducked down and pulled the trigger by accident, I heard a wretched scream and then there was silence.

Opening my eyes, I checked to see if any bullets she fired had hit me, there was no bruises on my body, I felt so relieved, my hand was trembling and so were my legs. I stood up from the carpet floor and noticed someone lying near the entrance door static, I rubbed my eyes and carefully approached the person. My eyes widened in horror when I managed to comprehend who it was. Lulu was sprawled out on the floor with blood spreading around her like a puddle outside, I examined where the leak was coming from and puked once I found the hole, her forehead had a small dark circle swirled with red crimson blood, her mouth was hanging open and her eyes were gazing up at me. Sweating tremendously, I waved my hand at her face hoping she would wake up, but I already knew what I had done, I was feeling nauseous again, I could not handle any of this, but deep down I knew I needed to do something about it. I accidently stumbled into the red puddle, some of the blood had gotten inside my mouth, I began to spit out all the excess like a mad man, this was not how it was supposed to be. Scrambling for the phone, I called the health care centre and the woman who responded asked me what seemed to be the problem. I did not even allow her to finish her question, my mouth began to blurt out everything from Lulu breaking into my house to Beatrice and her fighting to Lulu getting shot and now lying on the carpet floor not breathing. The woman told me to calm down and said they would send someone on their way to the house, all she wanted was the address which I gave almost instantly, I slammed the phone down and slowly fell to the floor staring at the dead body in the living room.

What had I done?

The tears came down my face like a sudden waterfall, I tried to wipe them away but they would not stop flowing, I bawled like a child who had just lost his parents; ironically, I had lost my parents. My father was dead, my mother was too far away for me to cling onto anymore, my sister was probably coming home right now, my grandfather was not in Germany anymore ever since my grandmother died five months ago, Beatrice was unconscious and Lulu was dead.

A day had passed since the incident, it was confirmed only a few hours after both Beatrice and Lulu were taken to the health centre. Beatrice was gradually recovering but Lulu had already died due to loss of too much blood. The people who were informed first were Marcus because Lulu was his cousin and me since I called in the first place. The man had come to my house and asked me with fury in his eyes what had happened, but he noticed that my eyes were empty and managed to shield his emotions. But before he left, he fell to the floor and broke down crying. My mother was there with my sister who was quiet and staring at me as if she knew what happened. I continued to stare at Marcus not knowing what to say, I mean what could I say? There was no way I could tell any of them the truth. What I explained to the police when they arrived was that Lulu broke into the house, knocked out Beatrice and then came to confess to me how she felt but when I rejected her, she immediately grabbed her pistol and shot herself in the head. I had to make it believable because if not then the police were going to come up with their own conclusions; Beatrice and I were suspects but a few days later the case was officially closed and it was ruled as a suicide, and both of us were let go. Marcus did not bother to contact me because he was heartbroken that his cousin was dead, my mother had decided to spend some nights with him while Beatrice, who had felt much healthier, began to stay for some nights with Mia and I since my mother was absent. The activities we did together were entertaining, but while Mia and Beatrice enjoyed themselves, I stayed in my room reminiscing what I had done to Lulu. It was going to haunt me forever and ever, and there was nothing I could about it.

Sleeping was another hassle for me too, the blood and the guns surrounding me as I saw Lulu aiming one in my face and firing consecutively woke me to a pool full of perspiration. One time I screamed as if my life was in danger, I kept scratching at my neck as if I had some creature crawling inside of me, digging and digging at my side until there was blood appearing on my fingers, and then the sobbing came again and again and again. This was becoming like an endless cycle and I was tired. The problem with murdering someone is that every time you wash your hands you only see the bloodstains on your palms and once you know you cannot wash it off you decide to try harder and wash more and more till your hands begin to sting. I had killed two people and they were both accidents caused by anger and fear, and what was the point of me feeling sorry for myself? I might as well be labelled as a murderer who had escaped judgement twice, a liar or fibber who had escaped the jaws of the law twice, a young man who was secretly a two-faced Jekyll and Hyde. I burst out laughing, grabbing hold of my face and staring at myself in the mirror, I did not know what was so hilarious but I just kept on laughing and then I stopped smiling and a sudden rage inside of me broke out. Smashing the mirror with my fist, I hit it again and again and again and again until my hands were bleeding, I could not even feel the pain, I had gone through so much that nothing could hurt me no more. The change of caring, being passionate, loving others was disappearing gradually and I understood that this was how it was supposed to be. I was becoming like him and was not noticing it, no not Hitler, more like M, the cold blue eyes were apparent, the scowling and the emptiness.

Is this what he was warning me about?

As I made my way back to my room, I bumped into my sister who was coming out of her room, she blocked my path and held onto my arms before pulling me towards her door. Mia then told me to sit down on her bed and folded her arms before scanning me inside out, she knew something was not right and she was right about that. That was undeniable.

"Matthew I will be very blunt with you, but you have acting different for the past few days. Beatrice and I are genuinely concerned, is there something bothering you?"

"Do not be concerned about me, I am fine, nothing is going on."

"Is it because of that incident? Is there something going on?"

"I TOLD YOU NOTHING IS WRONG WITH ME! JUST LEAVE ME ALONE!!"

"From your tone, I can tell something is wrong. Is it because you killed Louise?"

I rose to my feet and pushed my sister roughly against the wall, there was fear in her eyes as I raised my hand ready to slap her, but then when I felt her trembling, I let go of her and then opened her door and glared at her one last time before leaving. Closing the door to my room, I laid on my bed facing the ceiling before rubbing my red eyes, I did not know what my problem was, but if I did not keep myself away from Mia, I was going to do something that may hurt her. Emotionally and physically, I was not in the right place, it felt as if my whole mindset was evolving in front of my eyes and everyone else was falling further and further away from me, but it was better that way. It had to be.

CHAPTER 23

THE YEAR IS 1939, THREE years have passed since Matthew's supposed incident, but in Germany, the world was beginning to notice now Adolf Hitler's monstrous power among not just Eastern Europe but in Western Europe as well. Back in 1937, the meeting that had taken place a year before in Adolf Hitler's office had finally come into fruition, The Anti-Jewish Propaganda led by Joseph Goebbels had been eventually finalised. Throughout the year, the concentration camps that were built began to incarcerate "habitual criminals" left and right and all over Germany, anyone who had seen or heard of a person convicted of a new crime who was previously convicted of crimes were severely punished and joined in the herd of people being sent off to concentration camps too. Political prisoners were also sentenced to concentration camps because of their disobedience and slanders against Adolf Hitler and the Nazi Party, it was a horrendous year for anyone who had looted, stole from shops and even murdered anyone however not many criminals resisted these crimes against them. Some were proud of their acts which became very unsettling towards the general public. Goebbels stepped up the anti-Semitism propaganda with a travelling exhibition

Degenerate Art Exhibition called with the help of Adolf Zeigler and the Nazi Party in Munich from the 19th of July to 30th November. Once the Exhibition was built, the main agenda was to cast Jews as the enemy and it succeeded over time, half a million attended the extravaganza while some who went guessed worse would come of this. And they were right, hit the nail on the head, on the other hand, an English controversial politician called Winston Churchill criticized British relations with Germany, warning of something big. In his own words, he stated, "Great evils and racial religious intolerance", though many of his colleagues complained of his constant "harping on" about the Jewish civilians living in Germany.

In 1938, nothing was getting better in Germany for the Jews at all as Jewish persecution intensified severely. In March 1938, Germany invades Austria and conquers the borderlines and by September 1938 parts of Czechoslovakia are in their control too resulting in the expansion of Nazi territory. During September 1938, new territories are now under the regime of Nazi persecution, anyone who was Jewish or of Jewish ancestry were sent to either be put in trains to leave the country or put in prison for the time being to later be slaughtered and killed. In November 1938, attacks on Jewish businesses escalated resulting in ninety-one Jews dying and two hundred and sixty-seven synagogues being destroyed in a centrally coordinated plot which was passed off as spontaneous violence across Germany. Not only had the government turned a blind eye but they did not want anyone to question further on what the real reasons were and why it was acceptable because anyone who did was persecuted and thrown in jail.

A LOST SOUL: THE REVELATION

Later on, that month, thousands of Jews were sent to concentration camps by train, it became so packed that the railway stations had to be given more time to allow trains to leave early, Jews were only released if they agreed to leave Nazi territory just like the Nazis did in Czechoslovakia and Austria. Many did not bother to stay and argue and fled, during this time Matthew's relatives on his father's side had decided to leave too because they could not cope with the madness in Germany or else, they would eventually die. Meanwhile, in Britain, parliament agreed to house Jewish children and orphans managing to take in 10,000 minors but refused to change their policy for Jewish adults. As all of this was happening, the real fire was spreading in Germany as shops were destroyed, glasses were broken into and civilians were killed, this night was significant and was called Kristallnacht, the "Night of broken glass".

Time flies so quickly, the last time I remember being nineteen years old was almost three years ago, and now my birthday was tomorrow, I was going to be twenty-one. I had my own place now, a nice luminous but simple two-bedroom apartment all to myself, it was lovely. I bought the place at the start of the year. The month now was June and I was ready to let myself get prepared for a night out with my family, we were all going to visit a nice restaurant down in Berlin, I was living in Munich so it would be a mediocre drive from here, but I did not seem bothered by the matter. My mother had called me the day before saying that she wanted to throw a surprise for me, but I decided against it, that house had too many haunting memories I wanted to forget, it was until then we both agreed that we would all go out tomorrow which was today. I had not seen my sister since July 1938, I had travelled to Western Europe to discover new things and also rediscover myself as a person. Along the way back, I had bumped into Marcus Rhinestone who was not living in Berlin any more. During the three years that had passed we had figured out interesting information about my father. The fear of my mother being involved in my father's death had died down, but the men she had sent to protect him were Goebbels' men. They wanted to get my father's earnings from his successful business.

When he refused Goebbels had informed my mother to convince him, but my mother did not want any part of it, she eventually gave in and visited my father, yet my father still refused to do the deal. My mother threatened him that if he did not comply then Goebbels would send soldiers to my father's house. This is why my father kept babbling to me about him needing protection and having a weapon, it was when my father decided to take the offer everything went wrong. Goebbels was called and they met in my father's house, he had taken five men with him. A heated argument erupted within my father's house resulting in a fight to break out. One of the soldiers sliced my father's throat in self-defence as my father attempted to shoot Goebbels due to a sudden rage. But I knew there had to be more to the story.

Thinking back to receiving the information from one of Goebbels' men, who had been present when Marcus and I tracked his house down last year, made me not hate Goebbels, but only dislike his tactics. He could have handled the situation much better. The only people to blame were Goebbels and my father, the soldier that murdered my father was only protecting his employer, and if he did not, then my family and the remaining soldiers' families would have been persecuted by not only Adolf Hitler and the Nazis but the general public as well. My mother would have lost her position, and my family would have lost its honour. Not that it hasn't lost it already. I turned to the mirror and shook my damp hair, the curls I had were better off loosely shown, slicking my hair back was not the best option, but then an idea came to mind. I ran the water from the bath a few times through my hair before getting a purple hairband (originally belonging to my mother) and tying my hair in a knot. Staring at myself in the mirror, a few strands of my straight curls fell gracefully down my forehead but I did not mind, the new appearance was natural and made me look more mature than I ever was. I smiled to myself and buttoned my shirt before putting on my swastika symbol, it was a gift from my mother so I wore the emblem proudly, it was funny because, after the news of another victory in Eastern Europe, I was starting to understand what Hitler was trying to do all this time, he was slowly trying to reclaim the glory that Germany had lost all those years ago.

Once I hopped inside my vehicle, I switched on the engine and headed off to my next destination, Berlin. Along the ride I noticed more Jewish civilians huddling up like lost cattle along a large queue packed on the railway station. Gazing out my window during the traffic, a woman was holding the hand of her two children, the older one was a boy and the younger one was a girl. The girl lost her footing and slipped but her older brother luckily supported her and she smiled before holding onto his hand and following their mother towards the station. It reminded me of Mia and I when we would go with our mother and father to the store, but that was a long time ago, an awfully long time ago, I nodded and proceeded into continuing on my journey. The air breeze rushed past my hair as I stared at the people passing, the large buildings, the restaurants filled with buzzing crowds and the noise of the vehicles along the road. The memories of riding my bicycle back from school flooded into my consciousness, I missed those beautiful days, much quieter and peaceful compared to now, much more peaceful indeed. I made my way down my neighbourhood street and parked my car across the side-line, but then reversed back so I would not hit the edge of the pavement. I switched off the engine and pulled out my keys before hopping outside and shutting the front passenger door carefully. Buying cars weren't cheap, but I had the luxury of purchasing vehicles, however, I was very wary about damaging any vehicles I purchased because I did not like going through the costs.

Climbing up the steps, I turned to see if my bicycle was still there but it was not, it was my conscience playing at me again, I breathed in then out and knocked twice on the door. As soon as I was led in by Beatrice, I could tell there had been a few changes since I left. The living room had a new wooden floor and a much larger red carpet compared to the ones before, the chairs were replaced with white creamy ones with a style I had never seen in my life. The kitchen was redesigned with a dark grey background, but the dining room was the most unrecognisable, the brown polished table was now exchanged with a large, dark, oaked table. When I stared at the design, I could see weird patterns embedded in it. It appeared to be out of this world, futuristic if I could say for the least. I had not noticed the new chandelier hanging from the ceiling above me, shining like crystals and diamonds.

Beatrice escorted me upstairs to a particular room, I never expected to revisit this room till now, inside was my mother, who was doing her makeup, and a mysterious man that was wearing a military uniform. I screwed my eyes at him and he glared at me, I could tell that he did not like me and I felt the same. My mother stopped what she was doing and beamed at me before squeezing the life out of my body. Catching my breath, I forced a smile and she introduced me to the elephant in the room, his name was Ruberg Becker, he was bred and born on German soil, he came from Dortmund and had joined the SS military force a year ago.

Was he my mother's new man?

Mother noticed my scrutiny and quickly clarified that he was her bodyguard, Goebbels had insisted on her having one after what had happened with Louise. I made sure she quickly changed the topic. My head was beginning to throb just from hearing that name. My mother suddenly then added that she was allowed to choose any soldier that was physically pleasing to her, and from that sly comment I knew why she had really picked Mr Becker. I mean there was no denying it, he was an attractive man, but like the rest of the SS troops, they were all devilish in their own ways. And that was instinctively clear. I asked my mother where Mia was, to which she replied saying she had no clue, there was a sudden knock on the door, and Beatrice left us and headed straight downstairs. I heard a familiar voice and excused myself from my mother's room before following Beatrice down the stairs. I stopped myself halfway and noticed a woman wearing a purple bonnet and a white hat, her dress was dark blue and she had on purple stylish heels; she looked beautiful. Beatrice pointed at me and she followed Beatrice's finger, her eyes suddenly widened in excitement, and she took off her heels before sprinting up the stairs towards me. Once again, my life was squeezed out of me, just from the hug I knew who it was, there was no doubt about it, it was Mia.

Everyone was prepared to leave, but my mother was the last one downstairs, she was escorted inside her new vehicle, the wheels had a different shine compared to the last time I visited here. I wondered how much she paid to get them done. They seemed really expensive. Someone grabbed my suit from behind and I turned around to see Mia glowing at me and smiling, there was a prick of red showcasing on her rosy cheeks. Beatrice was coming as well, she was dressed in silky black with one black golden glove on her right hand, and she was also wearing heels, all the women present were wearing heels. I sighed to myself before getting into my car, but Mia was still tugging on my blazer.

"Mia, what seems to be matter now?"

"I told mother when you arrived that I am going in your car instead of hers."

"And she agreed? Are you sure?"

"Yes, yes, of course, I am sure, I will not lie to you."

"Oh ok, come inside princess."

Hurrying to the passenger door, I opened it and she slipped inside followed by Beatrice whom I did not expect to get in my car, but I shrugged it off and went inside the driver seat. The destination was only twenty minutes away so we had plenty of time, mother had booked us all seats for my occasion and even when I offered to pay, she rejected my offer. That was my mother for you, whenever it came it to Mia and I, we always came first. When we arrived, there was a large crowd near the door, I parked along the driveway opposite the restaurant while my mother's car went to park much further towards the place. Beatrice, Mia and I made our way towards the queued door with mother and Mr Becker, as soon as people recognised my mother, they parted ways and allowed us to go through. When we got to the checkpoint, a petite man guided us to a large table covered with flowers and a red velvet cloth, I grabbed onto my head feeling uneasy and dizzy, almost losing my footing. As everyone sat down, I queried with the man if there was a toilet around that I could use, he winked at me and pointed to the white oval door down the vast number of tables with the same colour stacked before me.

Avoiding looking at the tables, I hurried and squeezed my way through the noises and dramatic discussions wealthy men and women were talking about till I pushed the toilet door open and went inside the men's area. Staring at the mirror, I let the water run and threw some in my face to keep me sane, but it was not working, I tried doing it again but the colour red was playing in my mind. At the corner of my eye, I noticed a body laid on the floor, I turned around and got closer and drew back before grabbing onto the sink, it was Lulu, but I thought she was dead? I rubbed my eyes and opened them again, she was gone, I sighed, it was all my imagination, then the nauseousness in me began to rise substantially high, I put my head in the sink and vomited. I stared at the yellow liquid laid against the white smooth curved surface, I did not bother to rinse it off, I picked myself up and headed back to the table I came from.

CHAPTER 24

I DID NOT EVEN EXPECT this restaurant to be a major stigma for the Nazi party, when making my way back to the table, I saw picture frames of different individuals that I recognised from the office, there was Adolf Hitler, Joseph Goebbels and even Himmler. I dare say his full name. I used to, but after encountering him, he gave me that cold stare signifying that he would kill me if I ever addressed him informally ever again; the man was an animal. They were all animals; everyone I had encountered within the Nazi Party and even the German Reich were beasts not to be reckoned with. Once I found the table, Mia caught my eye when she sensed my return, she nudged me from across the table with her knee giving a concerned look. I beamed at her and nudged her back signalling that I was fine, but she was not buying it. Mia knew me inside out; why would I be surprised if she was worried about what was going on. It was inevitable for her not to be curious; it was in her genes after all and I was glad in a way as her maturity had increased dramatically. Usually, she would be dragging me during dinners to talk privately, but right now she just smiled and nodded before tending back to her meal. I was hardly hungry, I stared at my plate and noticed the juicy steak, potatoes and vegetables all laid neatly on the plate, the steam wavered to my nose, but I was not drawn in, maybe it was because I was tired of this reunion.

What was the point of this?

The only people enjoying themselves was my mother, Mr Becker, and Beatrice. Mia on the other hand was silent as she pressed her knife into the potatoes and cut delicately into the steak with ease.

"Matthew my darling, you have not even touched your meal yet, are you not hungry?"

Facing my mother with a fake smile, I lied to her about eating before I left Munich which surprised her, I just wanted to head back to my apartment and spend some quality time by myself, so I slyly wished everyone a nice day and began to prepare my leave from the table. Mother just stared at me not knowing what to say, before she could open her lips to speak, Mr Becker stood up and comforted her saying he will guide me back safely to my car, I tried to argue, however mother supported his suggestion. The man stared at me with a sinister look in his eyes, I shuddered, what was wrong with all these military soldiers? Putting his shoulder in my way while walking to the door, I moved three paces to the front so I could distance myself from him, I did not know what the man had up his sleeve, but I was not waiting to find out, we both crossed the road avoiding any collision with passing vehicles and headed towards my black car. Once I had reached it, I felt his hand close in on my shoulder, I smacked it away instantly throwing my fists up ready to counter, if necessary. Mr Becker tried to contain his laughter, he was covering his hand on his mouth and waved his hand away as he retreated to the restaurant, I sighed and turned back to the car. But when I was about to open the door, I sensed his presence once again and noticed his shadow closing in, I whipped around and blocked his punch and then followed with a clean uppercut to his chin. The man flew back but then shouldered me in my stomach throwing me off guard. I almost puked, falling to the floor gripping tightly to my stomach. Before I knew what was going on, my face was pressed against the window screen, his breath was strong and hot against my skin, I struggled to move my hand, but he was holding onto my right hand while my left hand was holding onto the edge of the car.

"You thought you could fight me; you are still a child, you have much to learn, but like I said, do you know what I do too little boys that misbehave?"

"Let me guess, you molest them."

I winced as he kept twisting my right arm backwards, the pain was excruciating but I bit onto my tongue so I would not scream. Causing a scene right now was not necessary.

"Once I break your arm, there will be no coming back from it, I do not think you understand that my experience in the SS distinguishes us."

"If you have the strength to break it, I would like to see you try, but you have my face pressed against the window screen so I will not be able to witness the spectacle."

"I see you have a smart mouth boy."

The pain was getting worse and worse, I closed my eyes waiting for the bone joint to pop, but I knew he was purposely taking his time, I could even hear his giggles in the background, my arm was screaming at me to do something, however there was nothing I could do except wait for it to happen.

"Matthew!! Matthew! Mr Becker, what are you doing?!"

That sounded like Mia's voice, I felt so relieved, Mr Becker instantly released my right arm and I knelt to the floor in agony holding it tightly. That was a close call.

"Erm......Miss Schmidt, I did not know you were outside, is the dinner party finished?"

"No, my mother was wondering why you were taking so long so she sent me to come and find you, and here you are fighting with my brother."

"I think there has been a misunderstanding, me and your brother were just playing around, that is all."

"We will see what my mother has to say about that, won't we Mr Becker? The only way you can redeem yourself is by making your way back to the restaurant. My mother will not be happy when I inform her what you have just done."

Mr Becker set off back to the restaurant and before crossing the road, he glared at me and proceeded to waltz inside, Mia fell on the floor and questioned me what had happened. As I revealed his intentions, a sudden rage overwhelmed her and she hit my car without thinking. Instantly I checked to see if there was a mark, but there was no scratch or dent. I exhaled and closed my eyes in respite.

"Did he think he could hurt you just because he sees you as a target? That man is sick and disgusting."

"Well, I will be gone by tomorrow so you do not need to worry."

"You are right, but one thing is for sure, you cannot drive back to Munich with a sore arm like that.
"

"I will be fine, do not worry, I will be able to drive, do not even try to come with an excuse to drive for me."

"Well, I do have an excuse now, wait here for a minute please."

Mia scurried back across the main road and sprinted inside towards entrance door, I stood up wondering what she had in mind, I took out my keys and unlocked the door before opening the driver seat and sitting down. Then I noticed her coming back and she explained to mother privately what had happened, and mother told her she will decide to fire the man, if need be. But to my dismay, mother also stated that Mia should drive me back to Munich because she did not want me to get into an accident. Well, if she knew me well enough, that was never going to happen, however in this case she might be correct, I was not going to bring risk to my wellbeing so I hopped out of the driver seat and gave Mia the keys. Mia, who was overjoyed by the matter, swiped them from my hand and quickly got inside before shutting the door. I went the opposite way and opened the passenger door before sliding inside. I had never been in a car with Mia before where she was driving, but I wished for the best and hoped nothing bad would happen to my car. The engine rumbled and the car slowly manoeuvred its way onto the main road waiting for passing cars to give leeway, Mia carefully made her way through the gap and the car suddenly sped off down the next exit towards the highway, I felt tranquil and relaxed, Munich was far away, yet we were going to get there safely. I had my doubts at times, but I trusted my sister.

"Erm Matthew, can I ask you a question if you do not mind."

"What is the question?"

"Well, I have not seen you for over a year, and I wanted to know what it is travelling to other countries like?"

"To be honest with you, it was a magnificent and wonderful experience, you meet new people, you learn different things that you would never expect to picture if you only lived here all your life. The food is superb, the cities and different faces, if I wanted to go again I would, and I will when the time is right. But not right now, my birthday is tomorrow and I just need to have some quality time to myself."

"We have not had any quality time in a while, I can stay for a day if you want, and you know we can go shopping, I can cook for you...."

"Mother would not allow it, and also do you not have school coming up soon?"

"Listen Matthew, I have been staying at Leon's place when I have the time, our mother does not worry too much, but I do get home on time."

"Leon? Is that your boyfriend or lover?"

"No......we are just close friends......nothing is going on."

"From your hesitation, I am going to agree with your lie, but we both know the truth, just be careful with these older men, some are only with you for..."

"I know, I know, you do not have to tell me, I am a grown-up too, I am 19 years old, stop lecturing me about the opposite sex."

I fell quiet, I had no response, I had to accept she was growing up and she was going to be twenty this year which meant more responsibility. I smiled to myself, I recall when she was only a few years younger, her maturity had evolved so much and I was so proud of her, I almost felt like shedding a tear.

CHAPTER 25

SO, IT WAS DECIDED. Mia was going to be staying with me for a couple of days after all the begging and convincing she had acted once we arrived at my place, I felt so guilty, but at the same time, she knew I was going to say yes. As soon as I unlocked the door, I escorted her inside and showed her around so she could understand where everything was. It was only a two-bedroom place but the tour took a progressively long time, Mia was the type of girl to note things down in her little notebook, she carried it around with her every time she entered into a new place of settlement. It all started when my mother had gifted her with it around the time my mother and father had divorced and gone their separate ways. Ever since that day, she would carry it with her like a journal and write down her experiences whether it be in school, going to new places, and even noting what was in those particular places for remembrance. I found it very odd when we were younger, however I began to acknowledge it more and more once I noticed how it helped her become smarter in situations; for example, when both Mia and I went to Beatrice's home for the first time back in 1933, upon her writing all the room names and equipment in the house, I had forgotten where the snacks were hidden. That was until Mia assisted me by checking her notes, the ones she had written earlier, reminding me of what room and cupboard it was placed in, and once I discovered she was right, her abilities have never been called into question.

I tried to enjoy my birthday once the next day came, but something in me was doubting everything till now, it was difficult after the dream I had the night before. It all started with the day Hitler had come to my house in 1930, I was thirteen years old, then it skipped to 1935 when I had killed the soldier with the hurdle, I was seventeen years old, and then 1936 when I had been captured by Marcus and Lulu. And in that same year, I had killed Lulu. I had woken up but this time I was not sweating or fearful, I was wondering why all of sudden before my birthday I had this dream, what was this sequence telling me? Was something terrible going to happen this year? And that was when my mood changed, that was when the feeling dawned on me, whatever M had told me three years ago in Jerusalem was coming back to me. He mentioned a cataclysmic event which would change history caused by none other than Adolf Hitler, but M failed to mention how it occurred.

What had M tried to tell me? What was the significance behind it all?

I scratched my head, I should have asked him to be more specific about it, I should have queried with him about what Hitler had done that had caused the world to turn upside down. Whenever it was going to happen, I was prepared, because my future self was not, I had a chance to change situations that M could not. I pressed my hands together and fell on my knees, the last time I had prayed was many years ago, but I still knew how it was done. No words were coming out, my lips were trembling, yet I knew that if I did not speak, the pain in my chest would not go away.

"I do not know if you are real or not, my father believed in you and taught me about you. My grandparents preached to my family about you. If you can hear me, I need a sign, I had a dream again about what my future self-explained vaguely to me three years ago, I just want to know when this catastrophic event will happen, please......"

I paused when I heard a sudden knock on my bedroom door, I hastily rose from the floor and opened the door to reveal my sister standing there with a broad smile on her face.

"Happy Birthday Matthew!"

I hugged her and held on to her tight, she vacillated before patting me on the back and ruffling my curly hair.

"Is everything okay Matthew? You seem so sad right now."

"Mia, I want to tell you something really important and promise me you will never forget these words."

"I will not brother, what do you want to say, I made breakfast, and the food will get cold if you do not hurry and eat."

"Promise me that whatever happens, that you will not die, promise me that you will stay alive."

"Where is this all coming from? But okay, I promise."

Letting her go, I brushed past her and made my way to the table to eat what she had prepared, I could smell it, the sweet aroma of pancakes, one of my favourites, seems like my sister knew me well. My mouth watered as I sat down and feasted upon the different plates and coloured bowls filled with delicacies and heavenly food: there was bacon, pancakes, baked bread, biscuits, eggs and last and not least cereal, which to my relief, was just cornflakes. Mia went to sit down on the chair opposite and giggled when I rubbed my hands together getting ready to devour the feast laid out before me, but as soon as I dug into the pancakes there was a knock on my door, and I signalled Mia to wait at the table and not make a sound. Heading towards the door warily, I went under my chair to pull out the pistol I had kept when killing Lulu, I had felt it necessary that it should be in safe hands. When I opened the door with the gun behind my waist, I sighed when I figured out who it was. Marcus Rhinestone. I mean he should have at least called before almost frightening me all over, he had only come to drop off a gift for me, he had a premiere to attend in Berlin which when I tried asking, he just put his finger to his lips and wished me a happy birthday. Luckily, he had not come inside my house, I trusted him, but deep down I knew it would be better if no one discovered my sister was here. The risk of losing her or her getting mixed up in anything unnecessary was out of the question, especially in the unprecedented times we were in. Germany was moving ahead, yet whether it was violence or bloodshed, people were getting hurt, including the Jews, there were hardly any Jewish people in Munich since they had been given a chance to leave the country. But the ones who could not leave due to their circumstances were still struggling tremendously, especially after what happened last year in November, that day was beyond horrible, it was sickening. I had just returned to Germany when I heard the devastating news. If my father, or even his parents were alive to witness everything happening in Germany, they would be disappointed.

A LOST SOUL: THE REVELATION

The time was now past 5:00 pm, the day so far was going perfect for the meantime excluding the dream and the prayer I had tried to accomplish in the morning. Breakfast was great, lunch had been splendid and now I was taking my sister out to eat in a nearby restaurant, which was only ten minutes away, I did not understand why I had to pay until she gave the excuse that she had put her "blood, sweat and tears" into cooking for me her best work, which meant breakfast and lunch. I almost laughed at that statement, I think she had forgotten that today was my birthday, not hers, but then again, I could not see myself cooking an extravagant meal like that for Mia because of two reasons. One is because I did not know how to cook and was never taught unlike Mia who learned from Beatrice, even mother baked treats for dessert when Beatrice had her days off in the past. And the second reason was because I had never had the time to do it, which was a sly excuse. When you were busy pushing yourself in the ranks of a dictatorship government where you had to earn respect and loyalty from the man in charge, you had no time to be learning how to make food in your spare time. It was funny because I had work coming up soon in the next few days, there was a deadline I had to get done, I had moved to another section, so I was not working under my mother anymore, I was working in a higher position, but my mother still had more power than me. And to get things clear, I had no competition with my mother due to the simple fact that she was family, but everyone had no chance, Karl had been "fired" for miscommunication of reports and affiliation with rival reporters who had tried to expose Hitler's policy plans. Back then, I did not know what gave him the idea to think it was necessary to do that, but after he was dismissed, the word spread throughout the offices, and we all knew that Karl and the reporters were sentenced to those concentration camps. The stories I had heard or shall I say the rumours were not the most pleasant.

Once we arrived there around 5:45 pm, we had already booked beforehand so there was no need to worry, compared to the restaurants in Berlin, the ones in Munich were more subtle and less packed with overcrowded civilians rushing to get inside. I pulled back Mia's chair allowing her space to sit down before winking at her to check the menu, she opened it up and her face glowed red when she realised the orders were similar to the first-ever restaurant mother, father, her and I had visited as a family; it was one of her favourites. The redecoration style was much more extravagant because the Nazis had decided to shower the swastika signs all over the place, but it was naturally built bigger and allowed more space for larger crowds when suitable. The tables were covered in a red tablecloth and the bottle of wine was laid in position at the front so we could easily pour away into our glasses. The red swirl of the wine was beautiful when poured, it was the colour, I tried not to think about it, I gulped it down and proceeded to order, including Mia, who was already fashionably waving her hand. During the whole process of waiting for our food to come, at the corner of my eye I caught a familiar face waltzing inside, I didn't even have to look twice to know who it was, it was none other than Joseph Goebbels, and he was wearing a dark tuxedo with a clean crisp white shirt and a neat bow tie. I turned my chair fully around so he could not recognise me, I had my hair in my bun so I doubted that he would approach me, instead of making myself obvious I pretended to drop my napkin and when I went to pick it up, I stared cautiously to see two men with him. I did not recognise them, they both appeared much younger than him, maybe they were acquaintances or just friends of his, I did not care to say the least, however, I was intrigued by how reserved they all looked. Mia, who noticed them, suddenly waved her hands and shouted Goebbels name, I almost knocked my head under the table.

What the hell was she doing?!

The man heard his name and his eyes met Mia's who was still waving, he signalled the men to follow and waved back smiling slyly, that was until he recognised me, he was even more impressed by how much I had grown, he patted me on the back and ordered the staff to get more chairs for him and his friends so they could join us.

The encounter could have well been avoided if Mia just kept her mouth closed, I think she had drunk more wine than she could handle, it was embarrassing the way she was talking and gibbering to the other men, she was all over the place. Goebbels snapped his fingers and ordered one of his men in the room to escort Mia to another preserved table, they carefully allowed her to stand up before taking her away. So those two men were not his friends but just his soldiers dressed in nice suits, very smart, he stared at me and cut into his meat before plopping it inside his mouth, he snapped his fingers again and an unknown lady, whom I didn't even see, came to sit down next to him.

Where had she come from?

The woman had appeared out of nowhere, which was odd. She was wearing a bright jewel piece around her neck which I knew from first glance was expensive, she was wearing a rouge dress from chest to bottom finished with shiny black shoes. The earrings hanging from her ear were ancient, but also had a luxurious touch to them. However, despite what she wore, it was her face that had caught my attention, she was much younger than Goebbels, incredibly beautiful and dazzling in appearance, from her eyebrows to her bright red lips; she was like a piece of art that Goebbels had on display. An art piece painted to perfection. I blushed as she sat down, she caught my gaze and her dark green eyes met with mine, I turned away quickly pulling at my collar, her hands rested on Goebbels side and she slid off her purple, brown fur coat that she had worn coming to the room. Goebbels sipped his wine and introduced the woman sitting next to him, her name was Bella Neumann, she was originally born in France but her family moved to Germany to settle when she was five years old, so most of her life she has been living in Germany. From her short brief story, her father was German and her mother was French, she is a model for the arts and there are pictures painted of her all over the galleries, however it was upon meeting Goebbels that took her career even further. I was not even listening, I was so stunned by her beauty, she was only twenty-five years old and through her career was known all over Germany. I was indeed impressed.

CHAPTER 26

STARING AT THE TIME, it was almost past ten, the day was closing in and it was getting late, there were hardly any people left in the restaurant, everyone had gone. My sister was cosied up in a chair resting her head on the table with her arms folded, she was tired so she took her time to get comfy on the table, the two men that were with Goebbels had been standing near the entrance watching if anyone else was coming in. If anyone watching from outside strolled in, they would get the message once they crossed paths. Miss Neumann rose from her seat and kissed Goebbels on the cheek before making her way back to the entrance door, one of the two men came and whispered in Goebbels's ear and he nodded telling them to make sure Bella Neumann made it safely back to her house. Once they had left, the owner came to offer Goebbels another wine bottle but he waved it away and thanked him for his hospitality. The owner bowed lowly and scurried towards the backway ordering his staff to clear the tables and get ready to shut down the restaurant. Goebbels stood up and patted me softly on my back, yet his face suddenly became serious and he sat back in his chair and relaxed a little. It seemed like he wanted to say something before he left, I did not know how long he was going to take, but I was not going to argue.

"Matthew, do you know about the Treaty of Versailles?"

"Yes sir, I do."

"And do you know why it is important to Germany?"

"Of course, sir."

"And why is that?"

The question threw me off-balance; I did not expect him to rebuttal my response with a question, but then again, I should have seen it coming. From the way things were looking for me, I had no choice. I wanted to prove myself, and here was my chance to do that:

"The treaty gave some German territories to neighbouring countries and placed other German territories under international supervision. In addition, Germany was stripped of its overseas colonies, its military capabilities were severely restricted, and it was required to pay war reparations to the Allied countries."

"Very good, I am indeed impressed, you really are a smart child, and I see why you are moving in the ranks. I am proud of you. But the reason I asked you that question is due to the fact that there is tension in the German Reich on why The Fuhrer is invading these certain countries. And to make things worse, these sudden questions are coming from our own."

"Why would there be tension?"

"Oh, The Fuhrer feels that some people under and the people who work under them are feeling uneasy on the certain direct moves we as a country are doing, where we are evolving and when we will achieve our goals. As you see I know you are not a part of these people because I would be very disappointed if you were."

"Of course, not sir, I would never question The Fuhrer's decisions or plans."

"Just making sure, and do not worry, as long as you are on our side and not their side you are in good hands, my boy. The world is changing and so is Germany, we are leaving an imprint in the soil and we will take back what we had lost in the past. The Fuhrer feels the same way, our territories are increasing day by day, month by month, year by year, the world knows who we are and we want them to continue knowing what we as a country stand for. Do you agree?"

"Yes......yes sir, I agree."

"Good, now I have matters to attend to so tell your mother I said hello......"

"I am living by myself sir, in Munich, my sister was here with me to celebrate my birthday today."

"Oh! Well, congratulations! I am indeed proud of you like you are my own child.... well, I need to head off, make sure your sister gets home safely."

"I will sir."

Goebbels rose from his seat the second time and stared into my eyes for the last time, I kept his gaze until he closed his eyes and signalled to the owner that he was leaving. Through the window, I saw the two men waiting next to a prestigious vehicle, it was something you could not buy here. I tipped the owner his money and noticed Goebbels had already left his tip there on the table before he had left, he truly was a different breed, I could never read what he was thinking. I confronted a sleeping Mia, and woke her up by nudging her arm, she squinted her eyes and smiled realising it was me, she let out a loud yawn and followed me to my vehicle. The time we got back to my apartment was 12:20 am, as I unlocked the door, Mia burst inside and went straight to her guest room and shut the door locking it from the inside. I could not blame her, yesterday had been a long day for both of us, luckily, I had no plans today so I could rest here and read some more books available on my shelf. Unbuttoning my collar, I went inside the fridge and took out a container full of water and poured it in one of the few spare glasses from the cupboard, the others were unwashed in the sink. I gulped it down and poured another one before thinking back to what Goebbels had said, he was right about one thing, Germany was trying to reclaim what was lost, but was the way Hitler approaching things the best way? I slapped myself hard on the face. This was exactly what Goebbels had warned me about, the people who were questioning his tactics would soon be dealt with soon or later. I did not want to be on that list. It would be unwise to try anything stupid, I let out a laugh, the younger me would have tried to handle the situation, but I was not the smartest back then compared to how I was now. Learning and experiencing new things within the government over the years had given me insight that unless there was someone more powerful than Hitler in Germany, no one against him had a chance. I washed the glass with soap and water, went to my room but made sure before that I had locked the front door. Ever since what I had experienced with Louise in the past, I was not taking any chances ever again. Paranoia had crept and latched onto me ever since, and I was glad that it had not left me. Closing my bedroom door, I jumped on my bed and lay there facing the ceiling, compared to my old room it was not a creamy white colour, it was hazelnut brown, I needed to sleep, I went to the window and gazed at the cars drifting in the night sky. Maybe staying in Germany was not the best option for me, maybe I needed to travel more often or just maybe I had to decide to think this further and leave this country once and for all.

The next morning, I received an urgent call from my mother concerning Beatrice, I was confused about what she was getting at until she bluntly stated that Beatrice had been missing since yesterday afternoon. The context was that she had gone out to get groceries in Berlin, but since mother arrived back home in the evening, she had not seen Beatrice at all. I listened to her while eyeing Mia who was eating her ready-made breakfast. As soon as my mother told me that I needed to urgently come and help, I agreed, promising that Beatrice would be found. After breakfast, I reported the information to Mia who indeed was petrified, I told her that she would not be staying here for the next two days, Beatrice was either lost or in danger. I did not want anything bad to happen to her. Rushing to my vehicle, I turned on the engine and waited patiently for Mia to make her way towards the car, I could not wait any longer, the more time we wasted, the more stressful it would be to discover her location. The drive back to Berlin was quicker than usual, maybe it was because I had accelerated much farther because of the bad news, I parked the car near the pavement and Mia slipped out of the car and started banging heavily on Beatrice's front door. No one answered, I got out of the car and asked individuals and neighbours close by if they had seen Beatrice coming around here or near the roads with the bags she had carried. Most of the responses were a no, however one of the neighbours said she did spot Beatrice hop inside a black vehicle with two men that she had not seen before when leaving her house. My mind brightened like a light bulb, this woman stated Beatrice had come back to her house from the store and was heading back to my mother's house, was she still carrying the groceries? Asking the woman what I was thinking about, she replied saying that she was still holding onto them, but there was a black bag she was carrying as well, I paused and processed what the black bag could be but my mind was dense. Thanking the neighbour, I recollected Mia who was standing anxiously on the edge of the road, we both hopped back into the car and I explained to her the key points of the conversation I just had with the neighbour. The one that was puzzling us was the black bag, whatever was inside was important and from the way, the neighbour described to me, it did not seem she was captured or forced to go with the two men, it was as if they had been waiting for her. The car was similar to my mother's car which meant that these people she was dealing with were wealthy, very wealthy, indeed. That meant our next stop was none other than our mother's house.

My mother was sitting by herself in the living room, there were tissues next to her, there were two men in the room as well, and in the far corner was Beatrice, her makeup was a mess and she was crying. So, they had found her, wait a minute, the neighbour said she left with two men, were these the people she was referring to or were they just relatives of Beatrice? Mia rushed towards a sobbing Beatrice and embraced her in her arms, I stared at mother who was not crying but she was heartbroken, something must have happened that has caused this amount of tension in the house. I went to sit down in the spare chair, but mother grabbed my arm and signalled to me she wanted to talk in private. I obediently nodded and followed her outside into the back garden; there was a window accessing the view of the living room and I could see one of the men offering Beatrice more tissue. Turning to face my mother who was twiddling her thumbs, I folded my arms and waited for her to say her peace but I noticed her hands were constantly shaking. Something was wrong.

"Matthew......When I had called you about Beatrice missing at the time, I received some devastating news...."

"What do you mean? How did you manage to find her?"

"Those two men in the living room work in one of the prisons in Germany, they came to talk to Beatrice which is why she had not been seen since yesterday."

"So, is this concerning her brother? What happened to him? Did he try to escape again?"

"No Matthew......he is dead......."

Did she just say Beatrice's younger brother was dead? My body froze and my mind exploded, I gripped my head and to my dismay, the loud ringing was echoing again. Another death.

"What.... How is that possible? Was he killed?"

"Beatrice's brother was sent to the concentration camps, and it was confirmed that he was shot by one of the guards by accident."

"AND YOU BELIEVE THAT NONSENSE?! THE MAN WAS KILLED ON PURPOSE!"

"From the reports, it stated that he got into a fight with one of the prisoners over food, one of the guards intervened and he began to fight the guard, one of the other soldiers warned him to stop but Beatrice's brother refused and attacked. A shot was fired and the man was on the floor dead. It was ruled tragic accident."

I could not believe what I was hearing, my mother knew it was no accident and so did I, she was just doing her role, she had no choice but to believe the reports, she worked for The Fuhrer even if she had been an investor in the past. I was no exception, I worked with them too, but the monstrosities were getting out of hand, and now Beatrice had lost her only sibling all because they hated criminals. And yes, criminals were despicable, but Beatrice's brother had nothing to do with crimes, he had been an editor in the past who had written nasty things about Hitler and tried to expose him through ex-members from the party and private resources. However, he had eventually been found out and arrested before being placed in jail, then the new regulations on all criminals to be sent to concentration camps became law, but now this. The story sounded odd, it was not adding up, maybe mother was hiding something she could not speak to me or anyone else about, I would not blame her because I did not want to risk her reputation or mine. I brushed past her and then stopped to question if he had any last words before he was shot, my mother had her back still turned so I could not see her face. All I heard from her lips was that he had yelled, "None of you people can take away my freedom" to the soldier, I tried not to cry because those words hit me like someone had thrown a brick at my heart. The man deserved better and so did Beatrice.

CHAPTER 27

I HAD DECIDED TO NOT return to Munich but stay with my mother and Mia. Beatrice hardly came back to the house because my mother had given her some time off to mourn for her now-dead brother. Mia was the one who usually visited her house and I dropped her there instead of her always walking the thirty-minute distance to the destination. Not only was Beatrice hurting, so was mother, Mia and I, we had met Beatrice's brother years ago before he was arrested, he was a genuine and considerate, but he did have a tantrum when it came to certain things like not agreeing on a specific subject or topic. Beatrice used to tell both Mia and I stories of what her and her brother would get up to which included stealing from shops, going to the gardens to gather flowers and most importantly staying up until they were tired writing stories. That was the stimulation of why her brother became an editor, while Beatrice loved to be around children, the older they got, the further apart they became causing a strain on their relationship as siblings. What never made sense to me was why my mother had hardly taken the time to go and check Beatrice at all, not only was it embarrassing for both Mia and I but it indicated that she did not want to confront Beatrice and tell her the truth of the matter.

So, I was going to do it myself.

As I parked my car and headed up the steps, I saw the neighbour I had talked to a few weeks ago standing outside on the pavement praying, I just watched her for some seconds before entering inside, what the hell was that about? Mia was the one who had opened the door and allowed me to enter Beatrice's bedroom, she was sitting there with her head down waiting for me. I had promised to have a short meeting about something I knew about her brother, Mia already knew because I discussed it with her prior, but I needed some alone time with Beatrice.

"Beatrice, I once again share my condolences, even though I did not know him as well as you did, it pains me too."

"Thank you, Matthew, I am gradually starting to accept the matter at hand but I have decided that moving on from it will be necessary even though it will be difficult."

"What I wanted to tell you is what I found out about your brother, on that day when those two men were with you, do you remember my mother taking me to the back garden at all?"

"Yes, I remember it very clearly, what did she tell you?"

"To put it as bluntly as I can, I believe your brother was purposely shot, and my mother knows this too which is why she has not visited you at all."

"How could you be so sure? The report said...."

"The report always lies Beatrice, you have to believe me, they will never tell you the truth, your brother was an editor who wrote horrible things about Hitler, he worked with men who had once been members of the Nazi Party to get information. Now let us be clear, do you think that Hitler has not read what your brother has written?"

"I......I think he probably has."

"Your brother was killed because he was a problem, putting him in jail was not helping and releasing him would not do any favours for the Nazis either. So, they had to stage a scene, make people believe it was an accident that just occurred, and they succeeded. I found out that the person who fought your brother was not even a criminal, he was another soldier that was paid to pretend to come up with an excuse to fight your brother. And once he was paid, it was stated that all he needed to do was distract your brother for a few minutes and pay one of the soldiers to "accidentally" shoot him, these people are not stupid Beatrice."

"Say what you say is true, how did you even find this information?"

"I work in the government, I have my resources but to be honest with you people talk behind closed doors, whether it be in meetings or office sessions, these people laugh at what they have done because they do not care. Everything is done to expand Nazi territory and our country is showing its true power."

"Does your mother know about this?"

"Beatrice, she should not know, but if you are talking about what I have told you, the truth, oh she already knew, she was probably one of the first to be informed."

"Well thank you, Matthew, I am profoundly grateful, I am, and for your mother, I hate to say it but I have lost respect for that woman. I already had ever since she allowed that devil into the house, when she divorced your father and now this."

"Believe me, my respect for her had been buried years ago, but she is still my mother and she is still your employer, so until then we both have to deal with her. Just promise me you will not tell anyone this."

"You have my word; I am not trying to risk losing my life either."

"Good, it is better for us to keep these secrets to ourselves."

I stood from the chair I was sitting on and went to hug Beatrice, she began sobbing again but no bawling or noises was coming from her, the anger in me was rising and most times I never knew why, but at this particular moment I did. There were many shady deals, prospective strategies, and most importantly corruption breeding within Germany. If I could do something about it I would, but what could a young man like me do? I was just one man against a whole country, yet again who was I to complain about life? I was living in luxury while people were being kicked out of their homes and living in poverty. There was a knock on the door, and Beatrice released me before wiping her eyes, Mia reappeared and whispered something in her ear, her eyes widened and she asked me to follow her downstairs. Without even checking who was at the front door, she opened it and there was the box, that Mia mentioned, left on the floor, she picked it up and brought it to the dining room. Beatrice warily stared at the box wondering to herself what was inside, something began to dawn on me that whatever was inside was not good news, Mia on the other hand, was smiling, curious of what it could be. Beatrice gulped and went to unopen the box but then she stopped and drew back. Pushing me forward, Beatrice wanted me to do the honours, she was scared like I was, she must have read my mind because she knew too that there was something in that box that was not right. Mia was scowling at the both of us and asked Beatrice willingly if she could open the box, Beatrice nodded slowly, Mia excitedly reached her hands on top of the box and opened the flap. I noticed the change in Mia's expression. Something was wrong. I could see her hands shaking tremendously and then she let out a scream knocking the box off the table, Beatrice and I stared in horror at a severed head rolling out the box. I did not believe it; this was someone's head. Beatrice, who was still trembling, picked it up by its hair and turned to see the face, her eyes started to water and she dropped it back on the floor before sobbing and clinging onto Mia. I went to check who it was and to my dismay, I realised it was none other than Beatrice's brother.

The eyes were hollow, it appeared to have been gouged out, his teeth were yellow and decayed, and his fair skin was ashy, how long had he been in this box? And who was sick enough to send this to Beatrice? Did mother know about this? I doubt she did, or had any involvement, was this from the higher-ups, or the soldiers who were paid to kill him? It was hard to pick and choose in this type of scenario, I examined the whole head from hair to neck, the cut from the neck had been clean that I knew it had to be by someone who was skilled with swords and knives. The person who gouged his eyes out was someone who had strong but small hands, and the rest of Beatrice's brother was just natural decomposition. It was so disgusting that when I smelt the box it almost caused me to puke on the carpet, Beatrice was still crying while Mia was in shock staring at the wall, she was whispering but I could not hear her. None of these people had seen a dead person before, none of them, it was Mia's first time and I was unsure about Beatrice but I doubted she had seen a display similar to this. I was not fazed by any of this. After killing two people, nothing in me was scared by deathly circumstance, it was like I was part of it.

What was I even saying?

I slapped myself twice on the cheeks and got myself together, the ringing was coming again, I needed to just breathe and relax, breathe and relax, breathe and relax. I opened my eyes and told Mia and Beatrice to shut up and listen carefully to me. Beatrice instantly stopped sobbing and Mia paused her speech before facing me with an emptiness in her eyes, there was a rage within me that was overwhelming and eating at my flesh, I had to control it before the beast let itself loose.

"All right both of you listen to me very carefully, I know this is incomprehensible and puzzling but the fact of the matter is that Beatrice's brother's head is in this house on the dining room floor. Beatrice, you are not safe here, and after what we discussed I hope you can now see that this is all real, these people do not play. You are permanently staying in my mother's house from now on, do you hear me? This is not me trying to persuade you, I am ordering you because your life is important to all of us and I do not want someone important to me dying again."

Beatrice wiped her eyes and told me that she was willing to listen to me, I exhaled slightly, finally, we were both on the same page. On the other hand, Mia was glaring at me, but deep down I knew it was in disgust at the people responsible for this behaviour. Matter of fact, we were all disgusted. And I noticed that her eyes were still glued on me. It was a murderous gaze that sent chills down my spine. She stood up from the sofa and made her way towards the head lying there on the carpet floor. Mia carefully put her foot over the head and asked Beatrice if she could destroy the "hideous figure on the floor", Beatrice hesitated before looking at me and I nodded, she wiped her eyes one more time before slowly nodding her head. Mia closed her eyes:

"I am sorry, I really am."

Her foot slammed into the head popping it like a pimple, the red liquid splattered on her face as blood oozed out, but she kept on stomping until she eventually crushed it, I turned Beatrice away and led her outside to my car. It was the best thing to do. Coming back into the house, the carpet was covered in red, from the walls to the floor, it was like the dining room had been painted crimson. Mia revealed herself with blood all over; her shoes were stained with blood, her shirt was dirty with blood, no, she was covered all in it. However, the grin on her face made me uneasy, she was smiling like some little demon who had just devoured its first feast, I was lost for words. She made her way to the car, but I put my hands on her shoulder and ordered her to change immediately. I was not going to risk losing my sister too. I guided her like a lost child up the stairs and offered to help take her clothes off, she came back to her senses immediately and slapped my hands away, I smiled. Mia instantly closed the bathroom door before making a weird facial expression. I did not know how to respond. I mean she had just crushed Beatrice's brother's head. As I waited outside, I decided to sneak into Beatrice's room to find any fitting dresses for Mia. That would be the priority for now.

CHAPTER 28

FIVE DAYS HAD PASSED since the incident, Beatrice was staying with my mother and Mia had finally returned to normal, but I knew that what my sister had done would scar her forever. I had returned to Munich, and resumed back to work, however I was afraid for Beatrice, every single day I wondered if she was okay and doing all right. What made things strange for me was that she was living with my mother, it was very unlikely but what if my mother was in on this? What if my mother was the one who sent the box to us through the man that knocked on the door? This was getting out of control, I was slowly losing my sanity and I was not realising it, I was crying out for help, yet I pushed my worries to the side. I was in my office room finishing off some documents to pass to Goebbels when I overheard something about the Nazi troops expanding upwards in central Europe. The military officers that had passed my office were talking about it really loudly. I had already heard that the troops were successfully taking control of all the central borders, but there were some small issues. I of course heard these small stories from Goebbels who invited me sometimes to just talk about life and he would slip these topics in without both of us realising. The more I spent time with him, the more I understood that he was one of the smartest men I had ever met in my twenty-one years of living so far, his intelligence in my opinion far exceeded any of the people I worked for, and he was one of them.

My only problem was how long could I keep this up? This whole act I promised myself two years ago that I would carry out to the very end, yet the more I learnt from Goebbels, the more I understood that if I continued to keep working in this environment, I will eventually become like them. Germany was growing economically and financially, but the ideals the German people currently possessed was leading the whole country astray. Would I ever leave this country? I didn't know. It reminded me when my father explicitly told me something about a scripture from the Bible, he read every single book including that, sometimes he would quote words from the Bible that I never took into consideration because I was too young to understand. He said:

"There will come a time where good is evil, and evil is good."

I did not get it back then but now after processing it in my head I understood what the scripture meant. This was a clear example of it and sadly I was living in the environment I deemed to hate, deemed to never be a part of all those years ago, however I was working for them, hanging and eating around them. I was too afraid to go against them after everything I witnessed. From my father to Beatrice's brother, I knew the power that the devil had was beyond anyone else in this country's control. I had been thinking about this deeply during a lunch meeting in Munich with Goebbels, I was trying to focus but I could not, accompanying us were two other associates from the same office I worked and the lovely Miss Neumann. I did not notice her gazing at me as I zoned in and out of the conversation, I excused myself to go to the toilet and I trudged through the crowd before stumbling into the male area. The only reason I had left was that I could not handle being caught by Goebbels not listening to him, he hated that, I had learnt that the difficult way a year ago when I first worked under him, it did not end well for me and my face. Gaping at my reflection, I poured water on my forehead and began to massage my cheeks, it was a technique I usually did when my stress was getting a hold of me, I washed my hands and opened the door but I paused when I recognised the woman blocking my way; it was as if she had been waiting for me ever since I had left the table. It was Miss Neumann. The woman grabbed my arm and dragged me towards the direction of the table. As we got there, I realised that everyone was ready to go. Releasing myself from her grip, I confronted Goebbels who had a bright smile on his face, I told him that I needed to head home because I had an urgent matter to attend to, he winked at me and asked if I could take Miss Neumann home because he also had business to attend to. I was about to refuse until she grabbed my arm and held onto it before softly answering for me. Goebbels chuckled before slapping me on the back and going with the three soldiers outside. I glared at Miss Neumann and she winked at me before escorting me outside pretending to know where my vehicle was.

During the ride, I asked her bluntly why she did not ask one of Goebbels men to take her home, she ignored me while putting red lipstick on her lips and blowing me a kiss. I knew that she was just trying to annoy me so I closed my mouth and kept on driving, she giggled and tapped me constantly, if there was one thing for certain Miss Neumann acted like a spoiled child. Bella Neumann lived not too far away from me which is probably the main reason why Goebbels insisted on me dropping her at her house, we arrived at the front driveway which had a wide stone step leading to the front door, I parked the car opposite as I entered through the dark black gate and turned the engine off. I got out of the car and opened the passenger door wide for her, she gazed at me and offered me a chance to have a quick drink with her before I set off to my "urgent destination", but I was no fool, Lulu was the first who had tried that tactic, and I immediately learnt my lesson. However, something in me was urging me to not waste my chances so I eventually gave in and she guided me inside her humble home. It was nothing special if I had to be honest with you, many houses in Germany belonged to the rich and wealthy. They all had similar formats and interior structures: the same style kitchens, stairs, hallways, dining rooms, and living rooms; the only thing different was that she had one room dedicated to just paintings of herself and her work. That was the first room she showed me when I came inside, she had two female servants standing awkwardly at the entrance, they were much older than her, no, that was not an exaggeration, they were really old, they could both be my grandmothers if possible. I was led inside the living room where I sat on the yellow golden sofa facing a painting showing a naked picture of a mother holding her child, Miss Neumann sat on the chair opposite which was a dark purple single chair with the legs brown and curved. Both of us were served wine by a mysterious-looking butler. I watched him as he poured both glasses, but when he left, I started to relax a little. My guard meter was rising slowly. As Miss Neumann sipped her second glass of wine, she suddenly began to speak to me softly:

"I hear good things about you from Joseph."

"Wait he talks about me to you?"

"Ah, not all the time but when praises should be given due, he does."

"I am very thankful; I do what I can to help our people."

"A very noble thing to say, but what I really want to talk about is two things."

"Go on, I am ready for anything you throw at me, Miss Neumann."

"Please Matthew, call me Bella, you do not have to be formal here, this is my house after all."

"Well....... Erm Bella....... I am prepared."

"Do you have anyone Matthew? Anyone you are seeing or romantically involved with?"

"Why is that any of your concern Miss Neu....... I mean Bella?"

"Well, to be honest with you Matthew, I have taken quite a liking to you, I am very bold when I talk about myself and how I feel. An interesting specimen."

"Well to be honest with you I am not romantically involved with anyone, but at the same time, I am not looking for anyone either."

"Charming as usual just like in the lunch meetings. And my second question is what do you think of Joseph?"

"Erm......Well I believe Mr Goebbels is an excellent person and very smart, he is helping this country evolve and is steering our country to artistic steps."

"You do not need to lie to me, I see the way you examine him, he is not here, hardly is, just tell me how you feel about him."

"Wait a minute....... Is he not your......? Erm......I do not know what to call you......are you two not together?"

"Oh no! Whatever gave you that idea! The man is almost twice my age, he is my mentor, but I cannot stop a man if he finds me attractive, I have been told that since I was a little girl. Do you not agree?"

"Yes, you are very beautiful but if you are not in a relationship why are you always associated with Mr Goebbels?"

"Well for business reasons, of course, he helps me further my career, and I help him claim artistic paintings of myself, it is a win for both of us. But you have not answered my question."

"To be honest with you if I may, I do not trust Mr Goebbels, however from what he has shown me I do trust him. Deep down I know what he is capable of......but that is beside the point......"

"What does that mean?"

"I.......... I cannot say.........I need to go but thank you for the wine."

Rising from my feet, I headed towards the door and then suddenly Bella came in my way blocking me once again. I did not have time for this nonsense. I aggressively pushed her out the way and she dramatically fell to the floor, one of the guards came in hearing her cry and grabbed me before I managed to reach the door handle, I punched him repeatedly in his face and knocked him out with an uppercut to his chin, he flew back landing on the table causing the table legs to break. Running through the main hall, I found the two maids standing at the door waiting for me, I waved my hand signalling them to get out of my way but they did not even budge; what the hell was going on? One of them suddenly revealed two guns from under her skirt outfit and began firing, I instantly saw the staircase and leapt right beside it to avoid getting hit. The bullets were bouncing left and right like two players serving in a tennis game, I squinted my eyes to see if they had stopped, but I could still hear the gunshots. I had not even taken my weapon with me, this was unexpected, to say the least, was I being set up?

I then heard the misfire when one of the guns needed reloading and used that to take my chance, I sprinted towards the first maid and swiped her legs with an under kick, she fell roughly releasing her grip on the pistol which rotated clockwise across the floor. I quickly picked it up and fired, hitting the second maid in her shoulder, she screamed in agony before dropping to the floor, it was for self-defence, if I had not shot first, she would have no doubt injured or killed me. I ran as quickly as I could to the entrance, but as soon as I opened the door a soldier hit me in the stomach and kneed me in my abdomen, I winced and let out a cry before dropping to the ground. I glared at the person and to my horror, I realised who it was, I recognised his face instantly, Ruberg Becker, what the hell was he doing here? The smile he gave me sent a rage up my spine, I stood and threw a lazy swing but he reversed and catapulted me back inside the hallway, I landed roughly on the floor, laying there static. Turning my head, I could see Bella towering over me smirking, I rose to get up but she pressed her heel on my leg causing me to yell; it was hurting my very being.

A LOST SOUL: THE REVELATION

"All right Bella that is enough, you do not have to keep going, give the boy some breathing space."

I recognised that voice. It could not be. No. I turned my head towards the entrance door and in walked the man I had just been talking about an hour ago, the man who had told me to take Bella Neumann back to her home, the man I respected the most, Joseph Goebbels. The man was wearing a different attire compared to the black suit he had worn at the lunch meeting, he raised his hand and snapped, Bella nodded and removed her heel, he snapped again and Mr Becker and two other soldiers rushed to me before pinning me down. I could feel the ropes burning me as they roughly tightened it around my wrists. I did not even struggle or resist, my mind was struggling to process why this was all happening, I did not know if this was a set-up, a test or just a sick joke, but whichever it was they had taken it too far. I glared at Bella who had a sad look on her face, it appeared to me that she never wanted any of this to happen, but she had to do it. Was taking her home all part of the ploy? The footsteps drew nearer and as the shadow was face to face with me, I looked up and gazed at Goebbels, he stared down at me smiling, it seemed so innocent, until his hand whizzed past me and struck my face. It was all a blur, I didn't even see it coming, I spat out the blood from my mouth and turned back to him in bewilderment, his facial expression had darkened.

What had I done to cause him to hit me?

Goebbels whipped himself around and headed to the living room, Bella followed behind him and I was dragged like a lost puppy on a leash to join them too.

CHAPTER 29

NO ONE IN THE LIVING room had spoken a word yet. The people present were Goebbels, Mr Becker, two extra soldiers, Bella Neumann, and me. The man I had punched in the living room prior had been escorted outside and the two maids I had injured were being treated in another spare room. My head was bleeding from the brutal fall I had faced when Mr Becker launched me back into the hallway, I knew he was strong but to pick me up and throw me with such force was indeed impressive. I was seated on the same couch that I had drunk my wine, only this time my hands were tied and my clothes were torn and badly manhandled, Goebbels was smoking a cigarette whilst staring out the window, he then turned to face me with the same expression he gave when we were in the hallway, there was contempt in his eyes. Mr Becker was standing near the entrance assisted by the first soldier, he had tried to keep a straight face, but he was enjoying every minute of this torture, and he kept rubbing his hands as if preparing for something that was about to occur. Bella had not even set her eyes on me; she was sitting in a single chair sipping her wine, but she eventually put it down and asked Goebbels if he could hurry up with this so-called interrogation. He ignored her and resumed back to the window. Eventually, after twenty minutes of silence, Goebbels went to sit down opposite me and passed one of his cigarettes in my direction, I refused because I did not smoke, he placed them back into his pocket and let out another puff before tapping down on a nearby ashtray.

"Now Matthew, I know you must be confused right now about what is going on so I will tell you. I have been given some information concerning a matter in the past that I believe has come to my attention to have been published on a certain paper, a newspaper, however it is yet to be released. And this rabbit hole all started with you and a particular person, bring him in."

The soldiers left the room and I heard ruffling and noises outside, my eyes widened when I saw them drag inside Marcus Rhinestone, they threw him on the floor and tied his hands before sitting on a singular chair allocated in the corner of the room. Marcus had been beaten up so horribly I could not even recognise his handsome face anymore, there was dried up blood on his ripped white shirt and his black trousers, I turned away when he recognised my face, this was all starting to add up. I knew from the instant I saw Marcus that this was about my father, what had Marcus done to get Goebbels to discover the truth? Something very stupid.

"You recognise that man Matthew? That is Marcus Rhinestone, the famous and known actor from all around the world, I guess you can say that is fate that drew him and I together."

"Yes, I know him."

"Of course, you know him, you were both working together, but what puzzles me is why Mr Rhinestone here thinks he can go to a publisher in Germany and try to write an article about how I murdered your father. It does not make sense does it, Matthew?"

"No......it does not."

Marcus Rhinestone blurted out that he would gladly do it again, Mr Becker went over and slapped him across his face before slapping him again and again. Goebbels raised his hand and ordered him to stop in which Mr Becker obliged, he glared at Marcus and spat twice on his face before walking back to his original position.

"C'mon Matthew, we all know that your father killed himself, that happened over three years ago, so why would you and your dear friend over there try to investigate further? Did I not teach you that curiosity is what killed the cat? Do you have anything to say for yourself?"

"I......I know you killed my father.........we learned the truth from two soldiers you fired because they had not done their job to prevent the whole situation from happening. I had taken time, yes, but I found out that you wanted my father's business to go bust, moreover, I found out that you wanted a percentage of his business to increase your propaganda campaign against the Jewish communities. The soldier you fired saved you from my father who was ready to kill you, yet you still seem ungrateful about it because you could not save yourself......"

I didn't even get to finish my sentence; Becky slapped me hard across the face without Goebbels's permission. I faced him, not fazed by his what he had just done, and he could see that. His eyes were full of rage and hatred and I closed my eyes waiting for him to do his worst. He pinned me down on the chair before striking me in the stomach, no one was stopping him. I tried my hardest to not show any pain or discomfort, and it was working. The more I did not respond, the less he began to strike me. He was exhausted for a while and eventually began to slow down before getting off of me and bowing low to Goebbels. He immediately left the living room. Goebbels was impressed that I had not done anything because he knew that I could not do anything, he stretched his legs and felt more intrigued by what had just happened and examined me for a while.

"So, you say all of this, that I killed your father, and so what if it is true Matthew? Your father deserved to die, not only did he refuse my offer but he was a Jew, and those people were deemed to be beneath us, and you know it."

"So, you admit to your soldier protecting your life by killing my father?"

"Oh, I do admit, I am proudly admitting it, to be honest with you your father was a troublesome piece of crap from the start, you should be proud that your mother was not there with us, I mean she was the one who offered me the deal."

"Wait......What do you mean offered you the deal?"

"I see, she did not even tell her son, that woman is full of surprises."

"What....... What did my mother do?"

"The offer I gave to your father was her doing, she was the one who suggested that brilliant plan, The Fuhrer wanted your father's business so your mother suggested doing a split share benefiting us in using the business for operations for our territorial bases. Then if he agreed we could secretly arrange a quick death for your father once we had full control, but sadly your father died too soon because of one of my men. I mean

I really have to thank your mother. To offer her ex-husband's business for our success is indeed splendid. I couldn't thank her enough."

Nothing came out of my mouth. So, my mother was the one who had suggested that my father's business would be essential for Hitler's plans.

All this time I had thought Goebbels was the mastermind behind my father's accidental death, but my mother had planned this all from the start.

Is that why she did not want me to visit my father anymore because she was planning to eventually get rid of him?

The government was going to kill my father eventually, even if he did the deal with them.

Why mother?

All this for what?

You would take down your own family to reach your personal goals? I thought back to what that innkeeper had told me when he mentioned he was glad my mother was dead, now I understood, I began to laugh hysterically. I did not know why but I just found everything said between Goebbels and I to be so amusing. I knew she was involved but this was all deeper than I expected and I had gone so deep in the rabbit hole that Goebbels now was giving me the carrots. I continued to laugh until my laughter turned into a dark fury and I leapt out of my chair and instantly headbutted Goebbels in his forehead, no one had expected it, Bella called her guards and they grappled me to the ground.

Goebbels touched his forehead and smirked, but he was just trying to conceal his anger. I began to let all my emotions out, I screamed, yelled, shouted, growled and threw insults at every single person in the room. They were all going to pay. All of them were going to get what they deserved, mother especially, my hatred grew and grew and I bit into one of the guard's arms. He instantly released his hold on me before drawing back. The other guard let go of me as well, everyone was scared, even Mr Becker, his hands were trembling. I had not even noticed that he had returned. To them I appeared not as Matthew Schmidt, no, I was a monster chained down by ropes ready to devour anyone in my path. The only calm person in the room was Goebbels, he was amused by my performance, but I noticed his legs were shaking too, Marcus Rhinestone was amazed by the situation. It was as if he was witnessing a work of art. Bella was the only one terrified to the core, she had kept her distance away from me but it was as if she saw something in me that triggered a memory because as soon as I hissed at her, she bolted out of the room calling for help. Goebbels ordered the two soldiers to take me away in his car, and put Marcus in the vehicle behind, they gripped onto me while I barked and snapped at them, Mr Becker was keeping his distance regretting ever laying his hands on me, he did not even need to say it, I could see it in his eyes. Wherever they were taking me I was prepared, I had lost all sense of happiness and joy, all my heart could feel was pain for one person, and that was my mother. I prayed at that moment as the vehicle drove off that she died a miserable death.

The destination we were heading to was anonymous, Marcus and I had no clue, he had been staring at me since we arrived. The place appeared to be an abandoned warehouse or an industrial building that was now abandoned or out of use. The windows were broken and smashed, the doors creaked and a few tables that we passed were destroyed and falling apart, even the machines designated around us were moulding and rusting. There was dried up blood on the walls which were full of webs and crawling insects, Marcus and I felt nauseous, yet my temper had subsided for a while since then, I realised that whatever had happened was now gone and mother would eventually get what she deserved since I knew what the future had in store for her. However, something in the back of my mind was warning me that whatever was coming was getting nearer and nearer, I just did not have the slightest clue when.

Goebbels went into a room and placed out two chairs for us to sit down on, Marcus was placed on the first one and I sat on the second one waiting for the soldiers to beat us to a pulp. Nothing happened. Goebbels examined us both and nodded to himself as if deciding a final thought. Facing me he began to speak:

"Matthew, I have decided not to kill you, it does not benefit me. I do not have the time to come up with another story for your mother and your sister. However, what I have decided is for you to leave this country and find another place to stay, and never come back here, do you understand me?"

"But what about my sister? What will you tell my family?"

"Simple. Your son has left the country and is going to travel or take a break, better than telling them you are leaving for good, that will not just make your sister curious but your mother too."

"And what about my position and my work?"

"Well, that is another thing, so I will erase your files and accounts; I'll tell the Fuhrer that you were not up to the task and I excluded you from it and then fired you from your role."

"And what about Marcus Rhinestone?"

"Ah yes, Mr Rhinestone, well I was thinking of killing him because the cover story will be much easier, but I have decided not to do that for similar reasons. The publisher is dead so there is no need to kill him, but I do warn you Mr Rhinestone that I specifically will be watching you at all times. If you even tell anyone, I will not be so nice and I may have to get rid of that person as well."

"Are you sure this is the right choice? Would it not be easier for you to get rid of us now like you did Beatrice's brother?"

"Ha, you really are a tough one to deal with Matthew and that is what I have always liked about you. I can kill you both now but like I said prior, it does not benefit me at all. Especially in your case Matthew."

"Were you the one that sent the parcel to Beatrice's home, the one with her brother's head inside?"

"Oh yes, I thought you would already have figured that out, I was the one who got him arrested with permission from The Fuhrer, but it was a warning for you and her if she ever tried to tell anyone the truth. Should I worry?"

"No, she will never tell a soul, I promise you that."

"Good, so this is what happens now, I will give you till tomorrow to get ready to leave for the train in the morning, my men will escort you there and give you a ticket. From there you decide where you want to go, as long as it is not in any territory of ours. Understood?"

"Yes sir."

Goebbels rose from his chair and snapped his fingers, the two soldiers accompanying us pulled us back to the direction of the doors and that was the last time I saw him. Before I left, a smile appeared on his face as he placed his cigarette in his mouth; I did not know if it was relief or if he was amused by everything that had occurred.

CHAPTER 30

THE JOURNEY THE DAY after was exactly as Goebbels foretold it to be, the month was still June, and I was at the train station with three soldiers all dressed in military uniform. I had two bags and my passport with me, the first guard in front of me pushed me roughly indicating that it was time to leave, I gazed at the train filled with civilians boarding. There was a sudden loud noise in the distance. Deep down I knew it was time to leave. I hopped inside while the three guards glared at me, watching until I had found a place to sit. As soon as the train departed, I relaxed and thought about how my life was going to be from here on out, I needed to find or buy a place once I made my way to America, I would get to Hamburg Airport and then travel there. Mother had relatives who lived in the U.S., my Aunt Jennifer, who was my mother's cousin, I had called her as soon as I was dropped back to my apartment yesterday, and she responded that she was happy for me to come and stay with her. From what she told me, my cousins were older now and were not in the house anymore so I did not need to worry about guest rooms or spacious living, even though my Aunt Jennifer was wealthy, she still used her family's name Schmidt which was not surprising. Before the call had ended, she said that it would be necessary if my mother knew I was coming, but I warned her that it would not be the wisest choice which she happily agreed on. I had visited my Aunt Jennifer when I was incredibly young, but I still remember how her house looked like, she was not just wealthy because of my family name, she had been an actress before becoming a land expert.

Over the years, she decided to expand her wealth by purchasing land in certain states, she was smart with her choices and wise with her decisions. Once I reached Hamburg Airport, I booked the next flight to Dallas which was where she was currently living, the plane journey there was not too difficult as the queues were not as packed compared to how it would usually be during the day. Throughout the journey, I thought about what Goebbels had said about letting me live, maybe he saw something in me that reminded him of himself but was just afraid to tell me; or was it a liking to me that he refused to let go?

I would never know.

Arriving in Dallas, I waited for a few minutes until I caught a woman with long, curly, blonde hair waving at me from outside the entrance, I recognised her immediately and headed outside embracing her in my arms. My aunt had not changed appearance-wise, but her voice had gotten a little bit deeper due to her strong accent, she had always lived in Texas but she had moved around the states until settling her main residence here, it did make perfect sense since this was where she belonged. There was a beautiful white car waiting for us, and the driver politely took my belongings before placing them in the back, I hopped inside and sat next to my Aunt Jennifer who was beaming at me whilst ruffling my hair. The house she stayed in was much different from the houses in Germany, they were much larger in size and she had these white styled poles built on the front which revealed the large brown double doors, with a golden case sign of her name on the side. The house I visited was the one in Los Angeles, I was around eleven or twelve years old, but this Dallas house was incredible! The waiter, who was present, showed me to my new bedroom, it was dazzling but it was the double-sized bed that caught my attention. The way it was positioned in the middle of the room and the bright colours that illuminated from the walls and windows reflected against it showcasing different colours, it was like I was staring at a piece of pure artwork. A few hours after I arrived, I had gone to explore the house and the garden so I would get used to the new settings, from the kitchen to the hallways, I instantly fell in love with everything I came across, I was just so thrilled to be finally away from the hell I had been enduring with for so long. Just the day before I had left for the railway station with the soldiers, I had asked my neighbours that same morning that same day to help me sell the property because I was never going to return. My neighbours were a couple who only lived a few minutes away, they were hesitant at first but once I told them that the money when bought would be theirs to keep if they wanted, they shook my hand overjoyed by the deal I had made. It was all I had, and now I was going to let it go because my new chapter was going to be much better than the last.

One night in my bedroom after struggling to sleep, I had tried to read the books that were displayed on the shelf, but none of them interested me. It was only when I finally had the urge to sleep that I had another nightmare. This one was a blur, yet I could hear someone calling my name, I did not know who it was. It felt devastating, I tried to cancel the voice, however it kept returning, the more I heard the voice, the more I could sense the person. I opened my eyes and I saw someone seated in the corner of my room, I felt scared, it was not a dream because I was in my bed, yet someone was in my room.

Who was it?

The mysterious person clapped his hands and the lights came on, I squinted my eyes due to the sudden brightness. The person then stood up and drew nearer to me till his face became a clearer view. My mouth dropped to the ground when I realised it was M, what was he doing here? How was it even possible for him to be here when the last time I saw him it was all an illusion, or was that just a part of my consciousness? The man ruffled my hair and grinned at me, I tried not to smile but I could not help it, I was happy I could see him again, to be more truthful I was glad he was even here, there had been something playing at the back of my mind and I was wondering what it was. M went to sit back down on the chair and he folded his arms. From the look of things, he appeared the same. I rubbed my eyes just to double check if I was still dreaming. He had on the black jacket, the hat, even his trousers and boots were all black, I smirked, he needed to upgrade his fashion sense. Opening his eyes, he coughed and pulled out a notebook before writing something inside.

"It has been a long-time boy, seems you have changed quite a bit, you appear to be much older than the last time I saw you."

"Yes, well......I was still a child back then, so times have changed."

"That is good to hear."

"But I have been putting your words into consideration."

"I can tell, I have been watching you from afar, and I am truly proud of you. However, I have come here to warn you about something that is coming sooner than you think. You felt it did you not?"

"Yes, I did, it has been messing with my head for a few days since I arrived here in Dallas, do you know what it is?"

"I do know but I cannot tell you the specifics, but I will tell you this before I leave you, do you remember when I told you that Adolf Hitler is planning to change the world, and will not succeed in the end, well you are about to find out soon enough what that change will be. My advice to you is this: everyone you knew in Germany, your sister, your maid, even your mother, your friends, they will suffer miserably and there will be nothing, and I mean nothing you can do to stop it."

"Wait......what do you mean suffer?"

"I have said too much, but it is time for me to go, my time is up, goodbye until we meet again...."

"Wait......M you cannot just say that and leave!! M!!"

I woke up with sweat dripping down my face, I wiped it off and my eyes wandered around my room, it was still dark, I sighed, it was just a dream. I could see the dark patches on my pillow, I needed to get a new one tomorrow, telling Aunt Jennifer that I stained the pillow again will cause problems. So, something was coming, but M mentioned that in the end people I knew in Germany would suffer, what did he mean by that? Maybe he was talking about mother, but he mentioned Mia and Beatrice, did they do something wrong too? I closed my eyes and tried to block the thoughts of them dying. No, that was not going to happen, Mia and Beatrice had to survive whatever was coming because Goebbels promised to protect them. Was it just me fooling myself? How could I trust that man after what he told me about what my mother had done? This was out of my control; it was selfish but I had no choice but to focus on myself. I gazed at the white ceiling. If only my father was alive to sort this problem out for me, why had I been so foolish?

There were much deeper things going on and I had only scratched the surface. If M was right about my family, I had to move on, my history with them had to be erased, I never considered myself a Schmidt, that name made me sick. If Aunt Jennifer knew what her cousin had done, she would have cut ties with her already but if she found out the truth, I would be putting her in harm's way, she would probably do something out of the ordinary and eventually Goebbels or my mother would find out which would lead to Aunt Jennifer's untimely death. I was not going to lose another person I cared about. First, it was father, then grandmother, then it was Lulu, and there was no way in hell I was going to put Aunt Jennifer's life on the line. I rose from my bed and got on my knees to pray, but then I paused and looked up at the ceiling in disgust, no, I was not going to do it, what was the point? After everything I faced so far, how would I know that there was not going to be more? Leaning against one of the walls, I thought about what my father had said about how the Israelites had faced slavery in Egypt and escaped because of a man named Moses. Whether that story was true or not, the parallel to now was so apparent, but my concern right now was who was the Moses that was going to save Germany from Hitler? From the looks of it, there was absolutely no one.

In September 1939, German forces under the control of Adolf Hitler bombarded Poland on land and from the air. Germany invaded Poland to regain the territory they had lost in the past during World War I and ultimately rule their neighbours to the east. The German invasion of Poland was a primer on how Hitler intended to wage war, this would eventually become the Blitzkrieg strategy. Germany's Blitzkrieg approach was characterized by extensive bombing early on to destroy the enemy's air capacity, railroads, communication lines and munitions dumps, followed by a massive land invasion with overwhelming numbers of troops, tanks and artillery.

After the German forces had devoured their way through, devastating a swath of territory, infantry moved in, picking off any remaining resistance. Once Hitler had a base of operations within the target country, he immediately began setting up security forces to annihilate all enemies of his Nazi ideology, whether racial, religious or political. Concentration camps for slave labourers, but mainly Jewish people in Nazi territories and Germany, were established for German rule of a conquered nation. Within one day of the German invasion of Poland, Hitler was already setting up SS "Death's Head" regiments to terrorize the populace.

SS had begun to develop plans to deport Jews to newly invaded Poland: first steps towards the systematic murder would follow after and in Poland, thousands of Jews and Poles were rounded up and shot which showcased the early indications of the Holocaust. Hitler approved a new programme of euthanasia to exterminate the handicapped and mentally ill. Meanwhile, war is declared on Germany by Neville Chamberlain, the Prime Minister of the United Kingdom, in support of their allies including France and other nations. What was determined was a primal example of leadership and terror, and Adolf Hitler was riding the wings high, the world was on a turning point and one thing was certain.

World War II had begun.

ACKNOWLEGEMENTS

I WOULD LIKE TO SPECIFICALLY thank three people who made this book possible: Rebecca Abiona, Dr Justine Baillie and my mother.

I would not have been able to get the work I needed done without the support of my mother. Her constant motivation and advice helped me to not only focus on completing this book, but knowing what to do with it as well.

This book would not have been completed if it had not been for the editing and proof reading of both Rebecca and Justine Baillie. I am grateful for Rebecca's suggestions and valuable contributions while editing the book. I am truly grateful for her input and will never forget it.

When it comes to the foreword, I have to thank my lecturer, Justine Baillie. Without Justine's feedback and contribution, there would have never been a foreword.

I am grateful to both my parents for their support and suggestions.

My mother always reminded me and said, "Miracle, what do you want to see happen with this book?" and I always tell her, "I want everyone who gets a chance to read it to enjoy it as much as I have."

Don't miss out!

Visit the website below and you can sign up to receive emails whenever Miracle Adebiyi publishes a new book. There's no charge and no obligation.

https://books2read.com/r/B-A-VEQV-MGQCC

BOOKS 2 READ

Connecting independent readers to independent writers.

About the Author

New-time author Miracle Adebiyi, born and raised in South London, grew up avidly reading adventure fiction and fantasy and watching movies like James Bond and Marvel whether with or without his family. His interest in writing stemmed not only from these books but also from watching historic documentaries and Anime.

Miracle always loved to draw characters from books and movies in school, church, and at home. It was not until during the lockdown period in 2020 did Miracle begin to take his writing seriously. He is now a full-time student at university studying English Literature and Creative Writing while also delving deep into his career as an author. In his spare time, he loves to listen to samples, whether old or new and create beats from them. He lives in South London, where he continues to write books about complicated characters.

If you enjoyed the book, I would love it if you can leave a review, it helps me and helps you.